EVE S
R HARRELL

HAUNTED
PEOPLE

A COLLECTION OF TRUE PARANORMAL ENCOUNTERS

CW01494793

Shadow people are a projection of our worst nightmares. Everyone has had a nightmare at one point of their life. But what if that nightmare was crouched next to your bed watching you sleep? A figure so terrifyingly darker than the unlit surroundings of your room. Shadow Beings come in different shapes and sizes. Some are horrid looking and stare on for what seems like an eternity, while others are misty-like and disappear in the blink of an eye. 15 spine-chilling tales of shadow entity encounters, sure to leave you awake past dawn.

★ ★ ★ ★ ★ "Absolutely Gripping." -
Dayna S.

★ ★ ★ ★ "A Captivating Page-Turner."
- Mike B.

★ ★ ★ ★ ★ "Worthy if it's own
podcast." - James Curro

★ ★ ★ ★ ★ "The Twilight Zone meets
Tales From the Crypt." - Liz J.

PARANORMAL STORIES OF HAUNTED HOTELS

20 creepy chapters to leave you craving more, from author Eve S Evans and R. Harrell.
Hotels are a place that some people frequent. Business trips, conferences, get-a-ways, and vacations. But these people have stories to share from their experiences at hotels that weren't quite what they expected...

As one patron has advised after a terrifying experience, if you are going to an unfamiliar area, ask about the history of the place before you stay there...

A Business trip with an unexpected ghostly twist and many others. Some hotel employees as well as patrons recount numerous terrifying paranormal experiences in Haunted Hotels.

★ ★ ★ ★ ★ "Absolutely Gripping." - Dayna S.

★ ★ ★ ★ "A Captivating Page-Turner." - Mike B.

★ ★ ★ ★ ★ "Worthy if it's own podcast." - James Curro

★ ★ ★ ★ ★ "The Twilight Zone meets Tales From the Crypt." - Liz J.

REAL CREEPY STORIES OF PARANORMAL ITEMS
HAUNTED
OBJECTS

Ever buy something second hand only to bring it home and notice odd things start to occur? After inheriting something old, did you start to feel off or watched? How about hearing or seeing things that just cannot be explained?

In this anthology of paranormal stories you will read about the most wicked hauntings that are assumed to be caused by haunted objects.

REAL GHOST STORIES
DISTURBING PARANORMAL STORIES
BASED ON TRUE EVENTS

Delectable variety of paranormal stories for the supernatural addict. Delve into the shadows and into a collection of stories so intriguing its binge-worthy.

Treat yourselves to a haunted apartment that refuses to be inhabited in My Very Own Place. Ever been the new kid at school? Well what about at a haunted school? Read more in New Kid, Old School. Never seek out antiques without researching the consequences first it never ends well. Learn more in The Collector.

★ ★ ★ ★ ★ "Not only does she bring the reality right to your face, but makes you experience what the person did in that situation. A home builder has many craftsmen, Even Evans needs no such help she creates normality out of the oddities of this world. She is a master writer!" – Slate Raven

★ ★ ★ ★ ★ "Eve Evans delves into the true "spirit" of things with this book. Collecting people's accounts of the paranormal. Evans does a great job in pulling in the reader with stories. Another must read for paranormal fans." – Kevin Killen

CHILLING GHOST STORIES
AN UNSETTLING ANTHOLOGY
OF TRUE GHOST STORIES

Everyone has had a nightmare at one point of their life. But what if that nightmare was crouched next to your bed watching you sleep? A figure so terrifyingly darker than the unlit surroundings of your room.

On some occasion or another we all have seen something out of the corner of our eyes and turned to do a double take. But what if, upon second glance, you come face to face with a being so hideous your blood turns to ice and your veins scream out in shock?

Some places contain secrets, others are local lore, but some have unimaginable truth behind the stories that echo throughout the world from their walls. If you delight in short stories that give you a case of the willies, then you will devour Chilling Ghost Stories in an instant.

After befriending a local homeless man, Annie begins having extreme paranormal activity in her apartment. Read more in: The Beggar.

Roger and his wife have saved for ages for the perfect home. Finally, they find an amazing deal on a local foreclosure. But what terrifying secrets are beyond its walls? Read more in: A Steal of A Deal.

Every summer is the highlight of her summer vacation when she gets to visit her grandparents for a few weeks. This summer is different. Something is lurking at her grandparent's home... waiting. Read more in: The Shadow Man.

Ever been scared in the middle of the night? Ever been fearful of the dark and what lies in wait? This young girl and her brother have an experience to last a lifetime. Read more in: Fear In The Hallway.
Delve into these stories and twenty more delectable paranormal encounters from paranormal horror author Eve S. Evans.

★ ★ ★ ★ ★ "Thank you so much for this book. It has helped me feel much better about what I'm going through. Thanks again!" – P. Jewels

Take your mind on a historic journey. Explore the stories and legends behind some of the world's most paranormal locations. Some of the tales you will find in this book involve: bloody apparitions, residual hauntings, objects moving by unseen forces, unexplainable temperature changes, entities on stairwells, a cursed road, a dungeon that held one hundred and fifty bodies and multiple other phenomenon.

★ ★ ★ ★ ★ "Facinating." – R Harrell

★ ★ ★ ★ ★ "Paranormal history at it's finest." – James Curro

VOICES FROM BEYOND
AN ANTHOLOGY OF LOVED ONES
WHO HAVE ATTEMPTED CONTACT
AFTER DEATH

A delicious assortment of enlightening paranormal anthologies for the supernatural enthusiast. These stories are a variety of true narratives from around the world where people believe they have been visited by either friends, family, lovers, or pets after death. After her twin's untimely passing, unexplained events begin to occur. With a broken heart she tries to mend the best she can. In the beginning, she shrugs off all of the unusual occurrences until she is forced to confront them head on and open her eyes to possibility. Maybe her twin is communicating with her from beyond. Read more in: A Twinly Goodbye. Barely out of high school, Lisa is thrown a curveball when her father suddenly passes. With her life now in utter chaos, he journeys to them with a message from beyond to ease the burden. Read more in: Daddy's Little Girl. A confusing late-night dream foretells of a saddening tragedy linked to their grandfather. Read more in: You Will Be Fine. After twelve years of love and memories, Anna had to bite the bullet and let her beloved Pomeranian go. But did she ever really leave? Anna begins to wonder after seeing and feeling unexplained events. Read more in: Here to Stay. A simple trip to the grocery store ended in absolute heartbreak after crossing paths with a drunk driver. With a shattered heart, she lets him go and slowly tries to heal. But it seems as if her son is not ready to go just yet. The first signs she ignores, but after a while she has no choice but to open her mind up to the possibility that he has never really left. Read more in: I Had to Let You Go.

★ ★ ★ ★ ★ "A light-hearted paranormal binge." – Trace N.

★ ★ ★ ★ ★ "Some of the stories actually made me tear up! I loved it!" – Brynn S.

★ ★ ★ ★ "Excellent." –Jorden P.

**TRUE GHOST STORIES
AND FRIGHTFUL TALES
VOLUME 1**

Whether you are a skeptic or a believer, at one point or another in our lives we are bound to experience something we cannot quite explain...

There are times where spirits can attach themselves to something whether it be an object, person or location. It could be an entity, energy, residue or just something far sinister.

Coming into contact with the paranormal can be both terrifying, and life changing. From furniture you brought into your home or a place you go to escape... you never know what could be waiting for you.

R. Harrell brings you a deep, somewhat disturbing dive into the minds of those afflicted by paranormal activity. A collection of True frightful tales sure to keep your delight for the paranormal satisfied.

The following stories are based on true events. Based does not intend to mean they are completely true events. Some of the stories in this book are from fact and some hearsay or stories told about a person, place, or thing over the years.

DEDICATION:

I dedicate this book to all
paranormal investigators,
mediums, psychics and all others
who openly help those who are
haunted. Thank you for all that
you do in a world we have yet to
fully understand.

-Eve

This book contains a collaboration of haunted stories based on true events.

The stories in this book are mostly hauntings that have happened around the world with numerous forms of haunted items or artifacts. Some are legends or stories and some are factual.

Please remember to leave a review after reading.

Follow Eve S. Evans on instagram: @eves.evansauthor

or

@foreverhauntedpodcast

Check out our Bone-Chilling Tales to keep you awake segment on youtube for more creepy, narrated haunted stories by Eve S Evans.

Let me know on Instagram that you wrote a review and I'll send you a free copy of one of my other books!

Check out Eve on a weekly basis on one of her many podcasting ventures. Forever Haunted, The Ghosts That Haunt Me with Eve Evans, or A Truly Haunted Podcast.

1 THe BANSHEE

It was 1983 when my wife was diagnosed with cancer. The doctors had said it was terminal; there was nothing we could do. I had to work full time in order to cover the medical bills, and I was struggling to take care of her on my own. Firmly against putting her in hospice care, we decided to temporarily move in with her parents. They would be able to provide extra care, and in the end, she would be surrounded by those she loved the most.

Shortly after moving in, my wife ended up contracting a slight cold, and we knew it might possibly mean the end for her. Her immune system was weakened severely from the cancer, and her body was not strong enough to fight against even a simple virus. I had taken an entire week off work to look after her and stay by her side with the hope of her getting over it. She had fought her illness this long, and I was desperate. She continued to do so, but I also knew I had to face the harsh reality of her eventual death.

It was late one evening when I was sitting by the side of her bed, reading the newspaper aloud to her until she drifted off to sleep. I kept glancing across at her, taking in the sickly pallor of her skin, the wan curve of her lips, until her eyelids began to flutter, and she eventually fell into a doze. I set down the newspaper and curled up in the armchair, watching as she tossed and turned in the bed, coughing every now and then. It was a horrible feeling, watching a loved one get sick, and knowing there was nothing you could do about it.

I was almost dozing off myself when something made me jolt upright. Someone had cried out. I immediately looked towards my wife, but she was still fast asleep, and there was no pain evident on her face. I waited for a second, listening out, but I didn't hear the noise again. I thought that perhaps I had dreamed it or mistook a different noise for something else.

I stood slowly from the chair, stretching out the cricks in my back, and went downstairs to make myself a cup of hot tea. I was wary of putting any lights on, not wanting to wake anyone else in the household, and fumbled blindly through the darkness to the kitchen. As I searched through the cupboards for the tea bags, my whole body froze. A chill settled on the back of my neck.

Someone was crying.

It was a harsh, lamenting sound. An unnatural wailing, the likes of which I had never heard before. The chill grew stronger, and goosebumps raised the skin of my arms. I glanced around me in a panic, rubbing at my bare arms as I tried to determine where the horrible crying was coming from.

For a moment, I wondered if my mother-in-law was being plagued by nightmares or something, but I was certain she was asleep upstairs. This noise sounded unnervingly close... and somehow, I knew it didn't belong to anyone in the house.

I crept out of the kitchen, barely making a sound as I moved on my tiptoes, and tried to follow the noise. It grew louder as I went through the front sitting room and towards the front door. Here, I froze. My breath formed a white specter in the chilled air. It was cold here. Unnaturally so. Definitely a few degrees lower than the rest of the house. The crying was louder too. It almost seemed as though it was coming directly from the other side of the door. It was a horrible, piercing wail, full of grief and sorrow, and I felt my own heart tremble in response to it. I was desperate to know who was making such an awful sound, yet part of me was also terrified of discovering the truth.

In the end, I managed to coax some courage into myself and moved forward, pressing my hands against the grainy wood of the door as though for support. I leaned tentatively towards the peephole and peered out.

The crying stopped almost immediately. My eye darted left then right, but there was nobody out there. It was dark, but I could see clearly that the porch was empty.

The silence that followed was heavy and unnatural after the constant sound of the wailing.

I hesitantly unlocked the door and pulled it open, intent on making sure there really was nobody out there. Almost as soon as the door was open, I felt something brush past me. It was like a cold blast of air, but one that only lasted a second, feeling almost clammy against my skin.

I spun around, looking behind me, expecting to see someone there. The hallway was empty other than the shadows clinging to the corners of the ceiling. But when I strained my ears over the rumble of traffic in the distance, I swore I could hear the soft pad of footsteps moving away from me. I hastily shut the door, making sure the lock was in place, and hurried back towards the kitchen, trying to make sense of what had just happened.

My hand went automatically towards the light switch this time, not wanting to be left in the dark, and for just a moment, as the bulb warmed up, I thought I saw something. It could have been my eyes playing tricks on me, but I was sure I had seen a face staring at me from the darkness. A woman's face, pale and thin. But when I stared, there was nothing there. I quickly concluded that I was simply tired. I had barely slept recently out of worry for my wife, and it was probably just my sleep-deprived imagination that was making me experience all of these strange things.

I returned to the kitchen table, sipping on my tea and reading the paper, trying to push away my lingering unease so that I could eventually get some sleep. But in my mind, I could still hear the echoes of that horrible wailing and feel the cold brush of air on my skin.

It must have been some time after midnight that I eventually dragged myself upstairs and got some sleep. It barely felt as though I had closed my eyes before I was being shaken awake again by a hand, gripping my shoulder.

My mother-in-law was stood by the side of my bed. Her cheeks were glistening with tears, and I could see she was finding it difficult to keep herself together. I quickly sat up and pulled her into a hug, already knowing the words she was about to say. My wife was gone.

"She's gone," she whispered with a shaky breath. "She passed peacefully, earlier this morning."

My own tears refused to shed, no matter how much I felt the pressure building up behind my eyes. In the end, I had known this was coming for a long time, but it didn't make it any easier to accept. My wife was gone.

I stayed with my parents-in-law until after the funeral, reluctant to leave them during this difficult time.

It was while I was packing my things to get ready to leave when I remembered the night of my wife's death and what I had experienced. Even now, I couldn't forget it. I ended up asking my father-in-law if I could speak to him and pulled him out of earshot of his wife. He asked me what was troubling me.

"The night my wife passed away," I began, unable to keep the wobble out of my voice. "I had an… experience. I could hear this horrible wailing throughout the house. I thought it might have been someone having a nightmare, but it didn't sound like anyone in the house. When I opened up the front door to see if anyone was outside, I felt something go past me, into the house. At the time, it felt like a cold wind, blowing inside, but it only lasted a second."

I expected my father-in-law to dismiss my words as nothing but the delusions of grief, so I was surprised when he began to nod. His face had taken on a solemn tinge.

"You heard the Banshee."

"The what?" I asked. I had never heard of the word, but the expression on his face was enough to bring another chill to my spine. Goosebumps raised the skin along my arms.

"The Banshee is a warning that death is approaching. It must have been attracted here by…" he was unable to finish, but I understood his meaning.

The Banshee had come because my wife's death was near.

What I had experienced was an omen. I didn't want to believe it, but there was no denying what I had experienced that night. I would never forget those unearthly wails.

2 CHOKING HAZARD

Working in a hospital, there is plenty of reason to believe that some sort of energy or spirits may be present there. Most people have heard strange sounds, felt strange sensations, or on rare occasions seen an apparition roaming the halls. On the other hand, my story is a bit different from the run of the mill experiences that you may have heard of. I am convinced that a shadow I saw in the halls one night led me to a person who would have died had I not been there at the exact right time. Is it a coincidence? Maybe, but either way, it is something I will never forget.

Early on in my career at the hospital, I tended to gravitate to the night shift. It wasn't that I liked the hours so much as the shift tended to be quieter than the days. You didn't have to deal with visitors going in and out, and most of the patients usually were asleep. However, not being a doctor or a nurse, I was doing paperwork or cleaning most of the time, neither of which bothered me in the least.

On this particular night, I was just finishing transporting an elderly man who had died to the morgue. It is one of the worst parts of the job since you can get attached to some of the people that have been there for a while. Although I hadn't talked much to this gentleman, I knew who he was and was sad for his family. They were regular visitors, and I would miss the small chats that we had.

The morgue is located in, of course, the basement of the building at the end of a long hallway. I had just hit the button for the elevator to take me back upstairs when I thought I heard footsteps coming up behind me. There are other rooms down here other than the one I was just in, but I hadn't seen any signs that any of them were occupied, so I was a little surprised but also relieved not to be alone. The place, despite being well lit, can be creepy when you're by yourself.

I turned around with a smile on my face to greet my coworker, but to my surprise, nobody was there. There wasn't any place for someone to duck into, and besides, I would have been able to hear the door open and shut, which I hadn't.

To relieve the butterflies in my stomach, I tried to convince myself I was hearing things. "Get yourself together, man. It's just your mind playing tricks on you."

Whether it was my self-talk or the ding of the elevator arriving, I managed to walk inside of the car without looking like a character from a horror flick fleeing from some unseen enemy. Once I got back to my floor, I sat down at my desk and busied myself with the mountain of paperwork that never seemed to get any smaller.

I was focused on the screen, but I could see the walkway out of the corner of my eye just in case someone came up to the counter to ask something of me. I see movement out of the corner of my eye, and I swivel the chair to see what they want, but I find the space in front of me empty. I get up out of my chair and start to look on the other side of the desk, thinking maybe a small kid might be hidden from view, but that isn't the case. Hands on my hips, I shake my head and start walking back to my desk.

From around the corner, I hear a voice call out. "Hey, over here, someone needs your help."

At first, I don't know if they're talking to me, but since I'm the only one around at the time, it is the only thing that makes sense. I take off at a quick walk and turn the corner where I thought the voice came from. I see a shadow dart around the corner, which didn't make sense because the only thing down that way was the employee breakroom and bathrooms. I was going to be upset if someone was just playing around and trying to get a laugh at my expense.

I turn the corner, and I see a girl of probably fifteen years old standing in the hall looking into the breakroom. I can only assume this is the person who was calling out for help. She is standing there staring at something on the floor, and I rush past to see if someone is hurt. On the ground, one of the nurses is clawing at her throat, and her face is an ugly shade of blue. I quickly realize she is choking on something and rush to give her the Heimlich maneuver.

After several hard inward thrusts, the food is dislodged from her windpipe, and her color begins to return to normal. I turn back to where the girl was standing a minute before, but the place where she stood was empty. I got up and walked to the door to see if she had walked down the hall, but no one was there. She may have just helped me save this woman's life, and she just took off; I couldn't understand why anyone would do that.

Turning back to the lady on the floor, I ask her if she thinks she can get up. She nods, and I bend down to give her some assistance. After she sits down in one of the chairs, I ask her if she had been eating with anyone or if she had recognized the girl that had been in the door before I had come in. She gave me a weird look and told me that there wasn't a girl when I came in, it had only been me. Try as I might to convince her otherwise, she swore that the only person that had been there was myself. I figured that she had just been in a panic and hadn't noticed her there. She thanked me profusely, saying that if I hadn't shown up when I did, she was sure she would have died.

I really wanted to find out who this girl was. For some reason, I was tired of the disappearing act that all these people were doing tonight, starting with the footsteps, the movement in front of the desk, and now this girl. I had a friend in security, so when I went on break later that night, I paid him a visit so he could rewind the tape so I could see where the girl had gone after I went in the breakroom.

Arriving at the front security desk, I greeted my colleague and told him what had happened. He stated that she had been lucky I came when I did, but I told him that luck had nothing to do with it. I explained what had happened and asked him if he could review the cameras on the floor to see if we could see where she had gone to.

He nodded. "Yeah, no problem. There's actually a couple of cameras that cover that area pretty well."

He hit a few keys, and up came the live feed of the floor. I could see the desk where I had been just a little while ago. He started rewinding the tape, and he got to the point where I had left my desk to see who had been standing there. At first, I didn't see anything on the tape, but when I looked closer, I saw a small glowing ball near the front of my desk. I asked him if it was some sort of glitch, but he seemed just as captivated by what he was seeing as I was.

We watch the little glowing ball fly away from the desk just before I got up and around the other side. I see myself turn my head towards the breakroom when I heard someone call out for help. I watch myself walk down the hall and turn the corner. At this point, we switch to another camera that looks down the hall to the breakroom. This is what I really wanted to see.

What I expect to see isn't what is on camera, though. Instead of the girl standing there staring at the choking woman, I see the glowing orb floating there, unmoving. I don't mean to, but I take a couple of steps back from the monitor. I don't believe what I'm seeing. I know what I saw, but this wasn't it. I almost don't want to look as I watch myself turn into the breakroom and disappear from view. I look on as the glowing ball flies out of the hall.

"That is the weirdest thing I've ever seen." My friend's statement is a major understatement.

Really at the time, I didn't know what to believe. I know I had seen the girl, that I didn't doubt, but what the camera recorded was far from what I had seen. What was that glowing ball? I had heard of orbs before this, but I'd never seen one before. As much as I didn't want to accept it, the only thing I could accept was this thing had led me to the woman in the breakroom that needed help.

I still don't know whether that orb was the spirit of the girl. I've asked myself that many times but haven't been able to come up with an answer that satisfies my curiosity completely. All I know is that woman may not be alive if it hadn't been there, and for that, I'm thankful.

3 BAD ACCIDENT

One day my partner Greg and I were on our way to do a wellness check on an elderly man that a neighbor had called about. They had been concerned if he was okay since he had failed to pick up his mail or newspaper the past four days. Most of the time, when we get these types of calls, it usually means someone is out of town and either forgot to stop the mail or just didn't have someone to pick it up for them. This wasn't always the case, though, sometimes someone was hurt badly, or worst-case scenario, they had passed away.

Pulling up to the front of the house, I could see why someone would be worried about whoever lived here. The mailbox was bordering on overflowing, and the newest paper had been left in the heap upon the step. The first sign that something was wrong was the porch light was on. Given it was the middle of the day, there was no need for it. Still, I didn't want to jump to any conclusions since I had seen people leave them on while they left town to make it look like someone was home. Knowing this, though, I couldn't help but notice the first bit of apprehension creep into the pit of my stomach.

Walking up to the front door, my partner, a uniformed police officer, knocked on the storm door, and we stood there for a second, listening for any footsteps that could indicate someone coming to meet us at the door. Thirty seconds passed without any sign that anyone was there. I reached out and pressed the doorbell, but no sound came from inside the home. I was starting to get a bad feeling about this check. If the person had passed away, it wouldn't have been the first time I had come into contact with someone who was deceased, but it was something that had never gotten easier for me.

Giving one last attempt at getting someone to hear us, my partner opened the screen door and knocked loudly. If someone was asleep in there, the loud banging that only a police officer can produce would surely awaken even the deepest sleeper. We stood there for nearly a minute longer before we walked away from the door.

"You want to walk around the house and look in the windows to see if we can find anything?" I asked him.

"Can't hurt." Typical chatty Greg.

He went around back while I started looking through the windows in the front of the house. If it weren't for the black and white that Greg drives to these things, we probably would have looked like a couple of guys looking to rob the place, but having the cruiser out front usually keeps people from calling in suspicious activity to dispatch.

I only made it past two windows and was looking into the living room before I saw something. A foot and the bottom part of the leg was sticking out from behind the couch. Guess we found our homeowner. I just hoped we were in time.

"Greg! I got something here!"

I see him walk around the corner. His face is unreadable, an expression also probably taught to people in his profession the same time they teach them how to knock.

He walks up to the window I'm standing in front of and looks in. "Damn. Doesn't look good."

We walk back up to the front door and try the handle; it's locked. I search under the pot near the door and am lucky enough to find a key hidden underneath. Unlocking the door, the unmistakable smell of decomposition hits me. It stings my nose and forces me to retreat a few steps to stop the rolling in my stomach. I reach into my pocket and pull out a container of vapor-rub. After the first time I went through this, Greg had told me about this trick for getting past the smell.

We walk into the living room, and I get the first look at the homeowner. His eyes are closed, and he is bloated from the gasses inside his body expanding inside of him. The guy hadn't been small anyway, but it gave the effect of a balloon being overfilled with air. We both exchanged glances. We know one of us has to check for a pulse that both of us know won't exist.

"I got the last one." He was right, but it didn't make it any better.

I take a knee next to the body and carefully press two fingers to the side of his neck. Up close, I can see the bruise that has formed near the floor where the blood has pooled under the skin, no longer being pumped, sending life, giving oxygen to the body. I carefully reach out and press my finger to the neck. It is spongy and cold. I probe a little, trying to find the jugular without pressing hard enough to risk puncturing the already straining skin.

Satisfied that the heart had stopped, Greg presses the button on the radio mic on his shoulder and calls for an ambulance to come and pick up the body. He gives them the details, and we start to walk towards the front door. Behind us, we hear the squeak of hinges and the sound of a door opening somewhere in the house.

With the unmistakable sound of approaching footsteps coming towards us, Greg pulls his sidearm, ready to face who is coming. I can't believe someone could have been living here with this old man and not called when he had died. I've seen a lot of things in this job, but the idea of someone doing that to another person sickens me.

I move behind Greg as we wait for whoever is here with us to come into view. The footsteps are in the kitchen now. It is like someone is just going about their normal routine while this guy lies dead in the next room. Greg advances silently forward, gun extended out in front of him.

Greg pulls his gun back to his chest and prepares to burst through the opening. I can see his mouth move as he counts to himself. Without warning, the door in front of him slams shut in his face. He jumps back and points his gun at the slab of wood and glass. He manages a quick look back at me. His eyes looked scared; the way they met mine seemed to ask if I just saw that.

The radio on Greg's shoulder beeps, and it causes me

to jump. A nervous laugh escapes my lips before I can stop it, and I try unsuccessfully to swallow the lump in my throat.

"Hey Greg, let's get out of here."

With a nod and a grunt of agreement, he backs out of the room, eyes never leaving the door. He doesn't turn around until we are back in the living room. I would have tripped over the body of the homeowner if Greg hadn't pulled my back at the last second. After the past few minutes, I had completely forgotten he was even there.

I walk through the door urgently needing to get some air. I double over as soon as I'm on the lawn. The oppressive atmosphere in the house has left me unsteady on my feet. I'm hyperventilating as I try and suck in air as quickly as I can. I get the feeling I'm going to throw up, and I have to spit into the grass. It takes me a couple of minutes, but I finally feel as if I can stand up straight without the nausea returning.

I have my hands on my head as I stare up at the sky. "What the hell happened in there?"

Greg comes up next to me and grabs hold of my shoulder. "You okay?"

I nod to him. "Yeah, I'll be fine. Greg, who shut the door back there?"

The blank cop stare is back on his face. "Tom, no one was on the other side of that door. There was no wind either."

It was more of a question than a statement of fact. He was asking if I could think of a reason why it happened. I couldn't come up with an answer that didn't lead me down a path that implied something I didn't want to consider. I took one more deep breath and dropped my hands to my sides.

The ambulance pulled up to the curb, and two paramedics climbed out of the vehicle. They pulled out the gurney and wheeled it up the driveway toward the open front door. Greg gives me a reassuring squeeze on the shoulder and walks into the house to help the paramedics remove the body

The body is loaded onto the ambulance, and it pulls away towards the hospital, where an autopsy will be performed to find out how the man had died. If I could have, I would have been long gone by now, but Greg and I are partners. Besides, he's my ride.

"Well, Tom, you ready to head out?" Greg already knows the answer to the question.

"Yeah, let's get out of here."

I look back to the house, now devoid of the person who had called it home. Now all that remained was the memories and things that you couldn't take with you when your time finally came.

My eyes pass over the window where I had first seen the foot and leg of the man who once lived here. From where I was standing, it looked like two glowing eyes stared back at the two of us.

I reached over and smacked Greg's arm. "Hey, do you see that?"

He looks at me then back at the house. "What?"

I point to where I'm looking. "There, in the window. It looks like two eyes."

His body seems to jerk a little, and I know he sees it too. We both stand there for a moment and stare, not sure what else to do.

This time I snap out of it first. "I think we should leave."

Without a word, he turns toward his car. As soon as he turns the ignition, he slams the car into drive, and we are screaming down the road, siren at full throat. He is in a hurry to get away from those glowing eyes in the window. Something is in that house. It could be that the man who lived there doesn't want to leave his home, or maybe there was something else there. I don't know for sure. Either way, it was determined to make its presence known to the two of us. That day we went into that house looking for the answer to the question of whether or not the man was okay, we came out with more questions, ones that I hope I never have to come in contact with again.

4 PHANTOM CALLER

The moon sat majestically in the night sky, surrounded by thousands of stars that reflected beautifully on the cold winter night. I wasn't a very big fan of night shifts, but I had learned to make the most of it every time I was on a night shift. I was flipping through the pages of a local magazine when a 911 call came in. I dropped the magazine immediately to attend to the call, but no one was on the other end of the line. I wondered why someone would call 911 and say nothing;

perhaps, the person was in a kind of distress or something. Without intending to assume, I decided to go check things out for myself.

The house was an old bungalow in a street that appeared deserted. Aside a light that shone through the window, I would have thought there was no one living in the house. I walked cautiously towards the door and planted a knock on it.

"This is the Police."

Seconds later, a confused looking pregnant lady opened the door. "Good evening, Officer."

"Good evening, lady."

"How may I be of help, please?"

"I got a distress call from this address. Did you call?"

"No, I didn't." The lady replied. She was constantly looking over her shoulder.

"Alright. The person wasn't saying anything, so I just thought I should check out the address. Is everything alright?"

"Thanks for your concern, Officer. I assure you that everything is alright."

"I'll just take my leave if that is the case."

The lady nodded and closed the door just as I turned to leave.

Another call came in from the same residence before I got back to the station. Was it some sort of prank? Again, there was no one on the other end of the phone. I sighed in frustration and turned to return to the house, making up my mind to ensure that I, at the very least, step inside the house to see things for myself.

The first sight that greeted me as I got back to the house was a pair of eyes peering out the blinds on the window by the front door. I put one of my hands instinctively on my holster as I planted two sharp knocks on the door. After waiting for close to two minutes without getting a response, I radioed for backup.

While waiting for backup, I turned the doorknob, and it surprisingly clicked open. I pulled out my gun and stepped quietly into the hallway.

From the hallway, I could hear the thumping of feet on the stone floor and the distinct sound of scuffling, gasping, and smothered screaming; apparently, two people were in a physical struggle.

Everywhere went silent all of a sudden. But the silence only lasted less than a minute before it was replaced by a sound rushing hurriedly through the air. It was accompanied by a heavy crashing thud in the depths of the house below.

Total silence enveloped the hall after that. Nothing moved. By this time, I was palsied with terror and began finding my way into the living room for the fear of the lady being in danger.

I saw nothing except furniture and fittings in the living room, but the whole way through the hall, I could bet that someone followed me; step by step, when I walked faster, it was left behind, and when I walked more slowly, it caught up with me. But never once did I look behind to see what or who it was.

I felt a cold chill of fright run around in my veins, not altogether as a result of the tense atmosphere, but nevertheless added its own horror. The forces against them, whatever it might be, was slowly robbing me of the will and determination that had brought me this far. There was real fear hanging precariously in the solemn atmosphere. But I still have to find the lady.

I held the gun straight ahead of me. I could clearly hear the blood as it flowed through my veins. Even my blood appeared to be scrambling for safety. There was another batch of silence, and it quickly became ever so deadly and then almost immediately, sounds were beginning very faintly to make themselves audible in the other parts of the house. Every time I focused my attention on these sounds, they ceased instantly. I silently prayed that the sound didn't come nearer and that backup arrived as soon as possible. Despite that, I could not rid myself of the idea that there was movement going on somewhere in the other parts of the house.

Backup arrived just in the nick of time. The house was secured, and with strength in numbers, we searched the rest of the house for anyone or the pregnant lady. In the first room we opened, we were half expecting to see someone facing us in the back room, but only darkness and cold air welcomed us. They went through the other rooms as well, finding nothing unusual. All was as dead silent as the grave. Without any iota of doubt, the rooms were absolutely empty, and the house remained infinitely still.

I turned my head towards the inner room, where I thought I heard something move swiftly. Without a reason to doubt it, we all knew that a sound of rushing feet was coming toward us. It was heavy and extraordinarily swift that at the next instant, the lights went out.

I saw a man's face just before the lights went out. The face thrust itself forward so close to my own that I could almost have touched it with my lips. It was a frightful face, bloody, with thick features and fiery blood-shot eyes. It had an evil expression written all over his terrifying face. He flashed his teeth as he thrust his head forward, revealing a set of scimitar-liked teeth.

There was no movement of air or anything for some seconds, only the sound of rushing feet was heard; the apparition of the face; and the almost simultaneous extinguishing of the lights. The lights came back on moments later. This time, there was no one in the room except us. No scary faced man or demon or whatever it was.

There was only one place left in the house to check, and summoning all the courage left in him, Jamie headed for the kitchen. The door to the kitchen was ajar, and within a few steps, he saw the woman on the kitchen floor unresponsive.

I couldn't tell if the woman was suffering from severe pregnancy complications or if she had been attacked by some mysterious creature, but what I knew for certain was that if we hadn't found her when we did, she probably would not have made it to the hospital alive.

Back at the station after our shift, Jamie and I finally talked about the odd rescue call. "I thought someone was in the house because I could have sworn I saw someone peering out when I arrived there the second time. The blinds were parted." I told Jamie.

"That's odd," Jamie replied, "because I too experienced something that I cannot explain. I saw a strange looking man just before the lights when out. And something even stranger happened."

"Yeah, what's that?"

"When you were over talking to fellow officers, I was helping to put her into the ambulance, and I felt a cold, swift breeze over my right shoulder. Then I could have sworn I heard someone whisper, 'Thank you,' directly into my ear. It gave me chills."

I sighed. We must have been lucky to come out of the house unscathed. This was unarguably my most scary moment as a police officer.

5 NOD FOR YES

It had been a fine day, but the evening was gloomy, and the darkness slowly crept up as the night grew old. I was sitting near the entrance of the precinct near the car park. My car's engine was still fired up as I just came back from duty. I was waiting for my coffee to arrive as my shift still had a couple of hours until it was over. I got dispatched two times that day, which, in my opinion, was a pretty fine day as I usually got way more duties than that. If only I knew that it was all going to change, then I never would've wished for my demons. The routine was pretty normal for me, and I was used to it. We got usual calls for thefts, violence, traffic emergencies, fires, and rarely homicide. But the call we received that day was the one that led to the weirdest and creepiest incident I had ever reported to, and that's why it still sticks with me. The call was not for any usual emergency; actually, the call was for nothing.

I remember sitting on the porch while sipping the coffee when the phone rang. The dispatcher on duty was my friend Jerome McMahon. I used to call him Jerry. Jerry was a quick learner and was very good at his job. We usually never got to listen to the calls firsthand as we had to be ready to leave for the scene, but for that one, I did get to experience it firsthand. I picked up the headphones to listen to the call while Jerry started talking. He asked, "911, What's your emergency?" but he never got a reply. The line was empty for a few seconds, while Jerry tried again. "Hello? Is there any trouble?... Are you okay?... Can you hear me?" We were used to being prank called and even the empty phone lines, but it was a rare sight for it to happen at this hour of the day as we were close to midnight. We even had instructions to hang up a call and not to keep the line busy for too long if the other side doesn't respond. So, Jerry had to hang up the call, but without wasting time any further, he started looking up the location of the call. If we don't get a response from the caller, we usually checkup the location of the call for any potential emergencies and do a wellness check, and that's what we did. We radioed for an officer to reach the location, but none of the officers were close enough to the location as compared to us. So, naturally, I had to be dispatched for the place and received the whereabouts on the computer in my car.

I was on my way to the location through the quiet passages, which were otherwise very busy roads jampacked with traffic. There were no sounds, and I couldn't even hear the engine with the windows rolled up, and the only voice I was hearing was Jerry's voice through the radios. He confirmed that there are no previous incidents from the location I was heading to, and I would be quite safe. I wasn't even stressed about the potential encounter before this information, but now I doubted my gut. It was as if Jerry put a seed in my head, which rapidly turned into a tree. I like to blame that on Jerry, but deep down, I think I had the same thoughts as him all along, which only surfaced on his statement. I shook it all off and traveled the rest of the way, trying to think about anything else. I reached the place, which was a house in a pretty normal neighborhood. I parked the car and wanted to bust into the place to check for any potential dangers, but I decided otherwise. I instinctively knocked on the door and, in a moment, a lady opened the long wooden door. She was wearing a robe, which was usually worn while giving birth to a newborn. It was very clear from the looks of it that the lady was pregnant.

I asked, "I am Officer Longstun. We got a call from here. Is everything alright?" It was clear that the lady was as clueless as me and, with a confused look, replied, "Oh, I think you're mistaken. I didn't call for any help."

I said, "Ma'am, I am pretty sure we got a call from your place.

I think somebody else must've dialed the number." She cut me off midsentence and tried to reassure "You're highly mistaken, officer. I live alone here. There's no one else who could've called." I didn't hear her this time. I wasn't listening anymore. My focus had shifted from her. I was trying to glance behind her in the hopes of finding someone and then hopefully saving the lady from anything she was going through. I had handled a domestic violence case before, and this one looked quite similar.

The victims didn't know how to properly communicate with the enforcement, and I found a perfectly good way for it. I told her to wait and that she has to sign something for me. I returned to my car and took out a paper and wrote, *'Are you being abused? Are you in danger? Nod for yes.'* I handed over the paper to her. She read it and shrugged and said, "I already told you, Officer, I am alright. There is no danger. Thanks for your concern, though, but I still think you must've been mistaken. I replied, "Alright then," and with that, I left the place.

I was in my car, driving back to the precinct. I got a signal on the radio about a call. That was the turning point for me that day. The night had already begun, but that was the point from where all the extraordinary stuff started happening. I wasn't able to experience this call firsthand, but Jerry told me about his experience, and I still shudder thinking about the possibilities relating to it. He recounted the instance to me about how he was sitting in front of his computer when he received a second call from the same location and how there was still nobody on the other end. This time, he waited for a couple of minutes before disconnecting the call in the hopes of finding a conclusion for the call but still came up empty-handed. He again sent the location to my computer for me to go back to check the place, but I didn't need it. The place was still very fresh in my memory, and I couldn't forget the dark alleyways I had to travel even if I wanted to. I stopped and turned the car around to once again start the expedition to one of the greatest adventures of my life.

I was once again on the same path, but now I dreaded it much more. It shouldn't have been so scary, but something about it kept me alert, and thinking about it still chills my core. I reached the place once again and parked the car at the same spot as before. I was careful this time and made sure that I didn't make any noise so that I didn't alert anyone about my presence.

I slowly approached the house's main entrance but was stopped dead in my tracks due to something that I just cannot explain. I saw a shadowy figure, or maybe it appeared to me like that, but I am quite sure that someone was there, peeking from behind the blinds by the door. It quickly moved out of its place as if it was alerted by my presence. I could sense my fear coming to life, and to keep it in check, I placed my hand on my holster. I was now ready for any encounter that could've taken place, but it still didn't mean that I wasn't terrified of the outcome. I again wanted to barge in, but my instincts wouldn't let me, so I knocked on the door and waited for an answer. A few seconds passed by, which seemed like an eternity to me, and I decided to knock again. When I still didn't get a response from the house, I called for backup.

I should've checked the surroundings first according to the protocol, but the thought of keeping a pregnant lady in danger for long or maybe she was the danger; I couldn't have been quite sure and did the only thing that would've provided me with some explanation. I tried to open the door with no hopes of getting it to open, but to my astonishment, the door quickly and quietly opened up. My consciousness was in a constant state of pressure, and it made me act quickly to ensure the lady's safety. I wanted to be more patient, but the situation demanded otherwise. I went against my will and called out for the lady. I tried one more time, but something in me knew that I wouldn't get an answer.

I again acted out quite the opposite of how I really am and walked rapidly to check the insides of the house to search for the lady.

I didn't try very hard because as soon as I reached the kitchen, I saw the lady lying unconscious on the cold kitchen floor. My first instinct was to take out my gun and keep it clocked for any potential threats. Once I was assured that I was alone in there with the lady, I quickly tried to wake her up. She wasn't responding. I tried to wake her up with water too, but it didn't work. The thoughts of giving her CPR came into my head, but she was pregnant, and the fact she was still breathing made me not do it. I was just on my heels, trying to make a decision, when I heard someone walk through the front door.

The backup had arrived. My fellow officers made sure that the surroundings were completely empty, and there were no signs of anyone breaking into the house. Once we were sure that no one was there, we took the lady to the hospital. It turns out that she was facing some very severe pregnancy complications, and if we hadn't arrived at the location on time, both the lives could've been in danger. I was relieved at the conclusion, but in the back of my head, I was still very restless. I couldn't figure out on the fact that we got two blank calls from the same location, and the calls weren't even much time apart. My fellow mate came up with a theory that she must've dialed the call and then, at the same time, fell unconscious. While it made a little sense to me, it still didn't explain the first unanswered call and the fact that we found no cellphone with the lady when she was lying on the ground. I was desperately longing for some answers, but I had no place to look for them.

Once we returned to the station, I was there talking to Mike, the fellow responder with me on duty and the one who came with the backup. I was there explaining to him about my weird experience. I said, "Hey Mikey, what do you think about last night? The weird 'lady' incident?" He quickly replied, "I am not sure what you mean about it, but yeah, the experience was a weird one for me too." I recounted, "I mean, the call came in twice and both times with no answer. I was the first respondent on the site... And then... I saw something that... I don't know." Mike was jumbled and keenly asked, "And then? What happened there?" I continued, "I don't know, I just thought someone else was there too. I could've sworn I saw someone peering out of the blinds, and they were even parted, which was a weird sight for me as it wasn't parted on the first time, and I am not sure she would've opened them that late." I paused for a bit. The look on Mike's face told me that he was waiting for me to continue, so I did. I said, "We even checked the place and found nobody. The house had only one entrance. I am also very amazed at the fact that I acted very differently." Mike asked, "Differently?"

"Yeah, it's hard to explain, but I don't think I was in control of myself last night. I was doing things against my will and even wanted to stop doing it, but something kept me going. I am not complaining right now as I am very satisfied that the lady is safe. But still, the incidents I recount are very hard for me to digest, and I desperately want some answers." Mike listened to my little rant, and suddenly his expression changed. It looked like he realized something, and it hit him pretty hard. He said, "Man, that's really very odd. It's not just about your encounter. I felt something too which made me feel very weird." I was surprised to hear that.

I was again getting restless and wanted to know very impatiently but waited for him to continue. He unfolded, "Remember when you told Pete and Roger to check the surroundings?" I nodded, and then he continued, "I was there helping to load the lady in the ambulance. As soon as I closed the ambulance's door, I felt a brisk pat on my right shoulder. It was like someone was congratulating me or us for our great effort to save the lady. I can't explain it. And oh, something else happened too. When I turned towards my right to check for someone…" I cut him off in between and said, "There was no one there," but he wasn't finished yet and replied, "Yeah, there wasn't, but then I very clearly heard someone saying 'thank you' directly in my left ear as if it was grateful to us for saving her. And again, there was nobody there. I don't know if it makes sense, and I didn't quite believe that it happened to me, but now hearing your experience, it gives me chills."

I nodded and didn't know what to say. I sat down, and Mike went to his office. I was there thinking about the incident and thought to myself, "I guess some things can't be explained..."

6 THE LIBRARY

One of the reasons I chose to become a librarian was because of my love of books. They were some of my best friends growing up. Losing myself in a story took me to faraway lands and adventures that only existed in my imagination. Sometimes though, truth really is stranger than fiction when over the course of a week me and one of my coworkers came into contact with something that I only thought existed in the stories I loved.

I had been working in this particular library for nearly a year. I had become close to one of the guys that were in charge of cataloging historical works in the building named Alex. Because of mutual interest, we became fast friends and tended to spend a lot of time together both on and off the clock. He was the first person to mention to me the fact that he was seeing a shadow figure roaming the stacks late at night when he was the only one here. Alex had a reputation for being a bit melodramatic, so I didn't really take what he was saying seriously.

Finally, one day he called in sick out of the blue. I had just talked to him on the phone earlier in the day, and he hadn't seemed like he had been feeling under the weather, but I guess it was possible for something to come on quickly. After my shift ended, I decided to stop by and see if he needed anything. When he answered the door, he didn't look well. It wasn't that he looked sick, just disheveled.

I remember specifically what he told me. "I can't take it anymore. Either I'm seeing things, or something is there..."

I had heard this same rant before, just not with so much emotion attached to it. Something had obviously disturbed my friend enough that he felt he needed to stay away from work. I knew he needed the money though, none of us made enough to miss much time, Alex included. He talked about how he was barely making ends meet as-is. Recognizing that my friend was in serious need, I told him that I would stay with him as long as he was there so he wouldn't be alone. He seemed unsure at first, whether that be for me or if he was willing to go back. I'm not sure, but in the end, he agreed and told me he would see me at work the next day.

Alex's shift was a couple of hours later than mine, so I decided to pick out a book to read. That way, I'd have something to entertain myself while he finished his work. When the library closed, I grabbed my book and went to the back room, where Alex's office was located. He was hunched over a number of old volumes trying to determine what pieces of information were relevant and what was not. As much as I love books, I'd hate his job. I read for the interest in a story; what he does seems too academic for my taste.

When he hears me come in, his head shoots up, and a look of panic is on his face. It drops almost immediately into the normal friendly smile, but I still saw it. He's still scared to even be here. I hope whatever he's dealing with, he can figure it out. I hate seeing him like this.

"I'm going to be a couple of hours. Is that okay?" His voice has an almost pleading tone to it.

I brush off his concern. "Yeah, it's all good Alex, take your time."

He goes back to work, and I sit down on a chair to read. I'm just getting into the story when I start hearing footsteps walking back and forth outside the door. We are supposed to be the only ones here, but it isn't uncommon for someone to lose track of time and find themselves stuck in the building after closing or a few teenagers just messing around. I get up and open the door to see the person out, but as soon as the door is open, not only do the footsteps stop, but when I look around for who was out there, the area is empty.

I take a couple of steps out to give myself a better view, but it doesn't change anything. The room is empty. "Great, now I'm hearing things."

I walk back into Alex's office and narrow my eyes at him, trying to act like I'm angry at him. "See, now all this talk of ghosts has me hearing things now."

From the look he gives me, he doesn't see the humor in my comment. I feel bad because I'm sure he thinks I'm making fun of him when in reality, I'm just trying to lighten the mood a little.

"Come on, Alex, I'm just kidding."

He ignores me and goes back to work. I pick back up my book, feeling stupid for what I'd said. I promised myself I'd be quiet until he said something. That way, I knew he wasn't mad at me anymore. I hadn't read an entire page, yet when the sound of the footsteps started up again. Rolling my eyes, I get up again to find out who is doing this.

I walk over to the door and turn the handle quickly and fling the door open ready to confront the person. To my left, I see a dark figure dart down a row of shelves. I charge after them, probably not my best decision, but I was already upset about making Alex mad, so I wanted someone to take it out on. The stowaway was the perfect target.

As I rush towards the row of books, I hear Alex yell something. "Kristi, don't..." But the words fade away as I turn the corner.

Charging down the aisle, I think I see the figure turn the corner, so I give chase. I've got them on the run; now I just need to catch them. I know this library better than most, so I take a route where I can cut the person off. When I get there, though, nobody is there. I can't hear anything either except the light panting of my own breath.

"That's weird. I know I saw them go this way."

I walked back to the only route they could have taken, but I didn't find anyone there. I went back to Alex's office so I could get him to help me find the person in the building. When I opened the door, Alex was bent over in a chair with his face in his hands. He looked up at me when I cleared my throat.

"Alex, I need your help finding this person, come on, it looks like you could use a distraction anyways."

He seems to deflate a little before speaking. "Kristi, don't bother looking for anyone. No one is here but the two of us."

"No, Alex, I saw someone running out there, now are you going to help me or not?" My tone was harsher than I wanted it to be, and I cringed as soon as the words left my mouth.

He didn't seem upset, though. "Kristi, I get that you saw something; I've seen it too. I've looked everywhere in this place already several times, but no matter what I do, I never find anybody. This is what I've been trying to tell you for the last week. There is something here."

"You mean *someone*, right?"

He shakes his head. "No, Kristi, I think there's a ghost in this building."

I didn't know what to say to that. Normally I would have thought he was messing with me, but he had never looked more serious in the entire time that I'd know him. He actually believes that what I'd seen was some sort of a spirit. I had already snapped at him once tonight, and telling him he was crazy didn't seem to be the thing to do here, so I just looked at the ground without saying a word.

The uncomfortable silence seemed to fill the space between us until he cracked first. "Kristi, say something. You believe me, right?"

"I believe you believe it, Alex. I don't know if I believe in ghosts, though. I'd never really had to up until this point."

The answer didn't seem to satisfy him, but he seemed content with the fact that I didn't dismiss what he had said completely. We went back into the office, and this time I left the door open, so I had an open view of the room outside. For the next hour, there were no footsteps or shadows darting away from the room. We both were on edge after the ghost comment and me running all over the building to no avail. I wanted to search the place top to bottom, but the prospect of coming face to face with a ghost as unlikely as it was didn't appeal to me.

Finally, he said he was ready to stop for the night, which was just fine with me. I was tired and hungry. He offered to buy me dinner, but I just wanted to get home and crash in front of the television for a couple of hours before bed. We hugged and parted ways for the day. He was off the next two days, but I restated my commitment to staying with him.

He gave me a smile. "Thanks, Kristi."

When Alex came back after his weekend, we spent several nights in a row together. Sometimes I would hear the footsteps, sometimes not. It felt like who or whatever this was, was toying with us. No matter what I did, though, I could never find anyone in the building. I was getting frustrated but was unwilling to totally accept Alex's theory of the ghost.

Then Saturday night came. We were in our usual spots, me with my book, Alex at his desk. We had just finished the pizza I had ordered, and I told him I was going to go out and finish organizing one of the aisles I had been working on early in the day. He seemed unsure if being alone was a good idea for either one of us, but all he did was smile and nod at me before turning back to what he was doing.

I had just finished with the first shelf and was starting on the second when I heard what sounded like stomping a few aisles down from where I was. It was louder than anything I had heard to this point, which put me on edge, but this was my chance to catch this troublemaker here and now. I darted around the corner and faced down the aisle where I had heard the noises coming from. I was expecting not to see anything which had become normal at this point. As soon as I took in what was before me, though, I wish that had been the case.

Floating in the middle of the aisle was what I could only describe as the shadow of a person. The form seemed to shift and change like smoke being blown about in the breeze, only to reform again. Its eyes were a glowing blue color that seemed illuminated from within. My entire body began to shake. Alex had been right, as unlikely as it had seemed. He was right. Slowly it began to advance towards me. I took a few steps backward, matching its pace keeping the space between us.

Suddenly it rushed towards me, I've never been a great runner, but at that point, I'm sure I could have given anyone a challenge. I turned and fled with every ounce of strength that I had. I could hear its footsteps behind me, gaining on me. I called out to Alex for help, but I didn't see or hear him anywhere. I was on my own, and the shadow was gaining ground. I did what I thought was my best option; I ran for the office. Nothing had happened in there, so maybe somehow it was safe. I figured my only hope was to get there before it caught me.

I turned a corner, and I saw the light on in the room; it was like a lighthouse in the fog. "Alex, help!"

He didn't answer. At this point, I noticed that I didn't hear the footfalls of the shadow behind me, but I wasn't going to risk a look just in case. I didn't know how a shadow could make a sound anyway. I ran through the doorway, grabbed the door, and slammed it shut, hoping that the shadow couldn't get it. I just hoped Alex was okay. Then from behind the desk, I hear a moaning sound. I rush around and see Alex on the ground clutching his chest.

Not knowing what else to do, I call the paramedics to get him some help. I know that I'm going to have to go out there to let them in, which means possibly facing the shadow once more. Alex is in trouble, though, so it isn't even tough to make the choice. When I hear the sirens outside, I rush out the door, key in hand, ready to let them in. It's a blur of motion, but they get Alex loaded up on a gurney and into the ambulance headed to the hospital. In the back of my mind, I know it is the ghost that did this to him, and I'm both furious and terrified that thing did this to him.

I follow behind in my car, wanting to make sure he is going to be okay. I hit the emergency room door and rush to the desk. The nurse there tells me I will have to wait but that a doctor will be with me as soon as they know something. Not being Alex's family, I know that I'm not likely to be given a lot of information, but I feel I need to be here. Not really sure what else to do, I call Alex's sister to tell her what has happened. Obviously, I leave out the part about the ghost. She says she is on her way, and she thanks me.

It takes a couple of hours, but finally, a doctor comes out and tells his sister and me that Alex is resting. He has had a heart attack, which at thirty-five seemed really young to me for something like that to happen. I seethe when I think about that thing back in the library doing this to him. I swear, somehow, I'm going to find a way to get rid of it.

When we're finally able to go back into the room where he is staying, he's awake and dismisses the severity of what has happened to him. Personally, I don't know how any heart issue is "minor", but he seems to be in good spirits considering what has just happened. I don't know how it is possible, but the stress of the last week seems to have melted off of him. He actually looks like my friend again.

His sister leaves after about fifteen minutes needing to get back to work. I can tell from the look that he gives me he wants to talk alone, so I tell her I was going to stick around for a while longer. When she leaves, I start falling all over myself, telling him the story of what I had seen and vowing revenge for that thing doing this to him. I apologize again and again for not believing him when he told me about the ghost and taking responsibility for him being here. I keep thinking that if I had believed him earlier that he wouldn't be here.

The entire time he just smiles at me and shakes his head. Finally, I can't take it anymore. "Why the hell do you keep doing that?"

"Alex, that ghost is the reason I'm here, but not for why you think." Now I'm really confused.

"So, when I had the heart attack, I saw something. It was the shadow, but it wasn't a shadow; it was a man. In fact, it was the soldier whose journal I've been studying for the past two weeks. He was a medic that was killed during World War I. I think that somehow his spirit has followed that journal. It wasn't until I think I was about to die that I could see what he truly was. I don't think he was chasing you, Kristi. I think he was trying to get you to come to me so that you could get me some help."

I didn't know how to respond to what he was saying to me. Was it possible that the shadow had brought me to him so I could call 911? He had been right about the ghost; could he be right about this too? So much had happened in the past week that I wasn't sure what to believe anymore.

After that night, there was no sign of the shadow roaming the building. I don't know if it was the spirit of the soldier that wrote the diary Alex was studying or something else. It did get me to the right place when I needed to be there, though, and for that, I'm thankful. I still work at that library, and it is strange to think that I now

have a story of my own that rivals
any of the ones that I read.

7 TOMBSTONE

Frustration had started to set in when my husband and I started looking for our first home. We were ready to move out of our apartment, but we needed to find the right place. Nothing had really spoken to us, and I could tell the realtor was starting to show signs of agitation. We weren't trying to be difficult, but I guess you could say we might have had unrealistic expectations of finding our forever home right away.

One day she called us and said she finally thought she had found the perfect place for the two of us. We had our doubts, but she seemed confident about her find, so we agreed to meet her there in a few hours.

Pulling up in front of the place, I immediately knew I was going to like it. It was blue and built in the Victorian style, complete with its own turret off to the left of the building. It had a small front yard with bushes and flowers and a small oak tree that provided a little shade. Something about it almost drew me in; weird as it sounds, the place already felt like home. I knew I wanted this place from the moment I stepped foot on the front walk. From the way my husband looked up at it, he seemed equally captivated by the house.

A wave of sadness passed through me because there was no

way we could possibly afford the home on our budget from the looks of it, and I wondered why we're being shown it in the first place. When I asked about this, the realtor told us that the seller had just put it on the market, and it was priced way below market value. She didn't know why, but from what she did know, the person hadn't owned the place very long. I just didn't understand why somebody would sell such a beautiful place after just moving in and at a loss to boot.

After doing a walk-through, I fell even more in love with the place. It was everything that I dreamed of in a home. We immediately put in an offer for the full asking price, which was accepted, and we moved in about three months later.

We had just finished unpacking and were going to put some of the extra things in the attic for storage. It was the one place in the house that we hadn't gone in yet. I wondered if we would find any treasures left behind from one of the previous owners up there. I peeked my head above the opening and was disappointed not to see stacks of boxes piled here and there. In fact, I didn't see anything in the space whatsoever. Then, I spotted a couple of boxes in the corner, and something white behind them propped against the wall.

Excited that I had something to check out, I hopped up and walked over to the boxes. I opened their lids and found nothing really of note, just some random odds and ends that you could find in just about any attic. All that was left was the white thing against the wall. When I first touched it, I realized it was stone, but it was warm. I briefly wondered about this, but realization dawned on me what this thing was. It was a gravestone, but why would it be up here in the attic?

I walked over and asked my husband to come up and help me. He climbed up, and I ushered him over to my newly found treasure. We lift it together to the center of the room and gently lay it down, so the carved writing is visible. It isn't just a gravestone but one of a soldier. It said he was a captain in World War I, and he had died only a few years after the war had ended. This further deepened the mystery of how this got here; this should be in a cemetery somewhere, not in the attic of some house.

The stone is too heavy for us to move safely downstairs, so we pick it up and put it back where we had found it and proceed to store the boxes that we had planned to put up there before I got distracted. It takes us about fifteen minutes, and we are done. We secure the piece of wood that closes the entrance to the attic, and for the next few weeks, the gravestone sort of fades from my memory. What would I do with it anyway? It wasn't something that I would display in my home for people to see, so I just figured that it would be best to just keep it upstairs.

The first strange thing that seemed to take place happened when I was getting ready for bed one evening. I hear heavy footsteps above my head that sound like they are coming from the attic. I could still hear the television on downstairs that was tuned to the football game my husband was watching when I left. He must have needed something up there and had gone up to retrieve it, but that idea quickly falls away when I hear the television turn off and footsteps coming up the stairs.

As soon as he walks into the room, the sounds above me go silent. This wasn't a new house by any means, and it had its share of creaks and groans, but this had clearly sounded like someone was walking up above my head. I told him what I had heard, but he dismissed my concerns with a wave of his hand. I got upset with him and told him I wanted him to go look to make sure. Now he was the one frustrated, but he went to get the ladder anyway because he knew I wouldn't drop the issue until it was done.

He returned armed with a flashlight and the ladder. He climbed up and looked around, but from what he could see, there wasn't anything up there but the boxes we had put up there. No trespasser was hiding in our attic, ready to jump out at us when we were sleeping. I felt foolish and a bit childish for making him go look, but my fears were gone, and I was able to fall asleep.

This wasn't a one-time incident, though. Every week or two, I would hear them, and it had become a point of contention between my spouse and me. I would always be alone when the sounds would start. It was like whatever was up there was toying with me. There was even a suggestion that I go and talk to someone. I didn't like what he was implying. Just because he hadn't heard it didn't mean it wasn't happening. I wasn't crazy, at least I didn't think so.

8 RETURN JUST TO LEAVE AGAIN

This happened to me just after me and my longtime boyfriend broke up. I had been cooped up in the house for almost a week feeling sorry for myself, basically avoiding everybody. I didn't want to hear people give me the "It's going to be okay" or "You're better off without him" speeches, so isolation seemed the best option. Really though, all it did was draw me down deeper into my sadness. I needed to get away for a few days, so I jumped online and booked a trip to LA for a long weekend.

After returning, I felt like a weight had dropped off my shoulders, and for the first time since the split, I saw the light at the end of the tunnel. Granted, I was still in the tunnel, but the end was in sight. I had gotten home late, so I just dumped my bag on the ground the moment the door was shut and locked. All I had planned for the evening was to call my mom and tell her that I had gotten home okay and then upstairs for a bath. I'd take care of the bag in the morning.

After making my call, I was all set to take a bath. The warm water would relax me, and I just knew I'd be asleep the moment my head hit the pillow. After dumping a generous amount of bath salts into the tub, I stripped off my clothes and sank into the warm luxury. I was just starting to relax when out of nowhere, I hear a loud banging coming from my front door. From the sound it made me feel like it might have been the police, or someone was really needing to speak with me. My bath ruined, I got out, toweled off, and put on a quick change of clothes. The entire time the knocking continued gaining in both pace and sound.

"Hold on. I'm coming!" I yelled as I entered the living room.

As soon as I caught sight of the door, though, the knocking stopped immediately. I know I had yelled that I was on my way, but to have someone this insistent that they would continue knocking for nearly five minutes then to abruptly stop made me a bit uneasy. I walked up to my door and stuck my hand out, ready to unlatch the door, but the moment my hand touched the lock, the hairs on the back of my neck stood on end. Call it intuition or whatever, but something was telling me that I didn't want to open the door for some reason.

Instead, I reached over and flipped on the porch light and pushed aside the blinds to see if I could tell who was outside. Moving my head back and forth, I surveyed the front step, but I didn't see anyone. I squinted to see out to my driveway, but once again, nobody was there either. I started to get a really bad feeling about what was going on, enough so that I started to shiver.

I pulled my cell phone out of my pocket and hit the speed dial for my mom. She answered on the second ring, asking me if I was okay. It wasn't normal for me to be calling back like this unless something was wrong. I told her what had happened, and she said to make sure all the windows and doors were locked. She stayed on the phone as I went around my house and checked.

Once satisfied that every entrance was secure, I went back to my bedroom and sat down on my bed. My room has always been a place where I feel safe, but for some reason, tonight, this didn't seem to be the case. I told my mom I needed her to come and get me. She lived almost thirty minutes away, and it was already pretty late, but my mom didn't hesitate to tell me she was on her way. I thanked her and hung up the phone.

I laid back onto my comforter and tried to take a few steadying breaths to calm my nerves. I began to hear a rattling noise coming from the other side of the room. I looked over and noticed it was coming from the direction of my closet. The door handle slowly started to turn on its own and emitted a soft click as the door swung open about three or four inches. I sat there staring at it, expecting someone to burst out at any moment. I had a quick thought of whether I should call 911 or if I screamed if my neighbors would hear me.

I probably sat there for thirty seconds, waiting for the worst, too paralyzed by fear to do anything but look. Finally, though, I couldn't wait any longer. The smart move would have been to just get up and leave, but I had to know if someone was in my house. As I got closer and closer, I started to get dizzy, but I was determined to see who was in my closet. I walked up and grabbed the handle. I told myself it was like a band-aid; just do it quickly and get it over with.

With a quick jerk, I swung the door open, and it banged hard against the wall, making me jump. After recovering from the initial shock, I peered into the small area in front of me, Empty, but how could that be? It had opened, the knob had turned, I'd seen it, I'd heard it.

Now I was getting really freaked out. I grabbed my phone and car keys and ran for the front door. My mom was on her way, but I'd call her and tell her I'd meet her somewhere. I wasn't going to wait for her.

I ended up going back to my house the next day. As scared as I had been the night before, it was still my home. From what I've been able to gather, some spirits are attracted to negative emotions. Until I returned home from my trip, there had been plenty of that and some to spare in that place. A lot of people have heard the saying "Haunted by ghosts of the past". I think that something had been feeding on all the negativity I had felt before I left, and it had been waiting for me or just happened to be there when I got back.

Since then, I did a cleansing of all the rooms. I haven't seen or experienced any strange or supernatural occurrences since that night. But one thing is for sure, it is something I'll never forget, and it taught me a lesson that I had to learn the hard way.

9 SOMETHING FOLLOWED ME HOME

I've always been an adrenaline junkie. ATV's, dirt bikes, you name it, I've got one. I can't think of anything more fun than taking one of these machines out in the mountains near my home and exploring places that I've never been before. Most days, I don't see anything but the beautiful scenery of the country around me, which is never a disappointment. Other times I might find something new that just makes me appreciate where I live that much more. This, though, is a story about me finding something that I wish I never had because ever since that day two months ago, my life appears that it will never be the same again.

One of my friends had told me about a new trail that he had found up in the mountains above his house. He assumed correctly that I would like to join him in investigating this new location. He told me that it was a single lane trail, so we decided to ride our dirt bikes up to see what we could find. We planned on meeting up the next day at around 5:00 pm to begin our trip up.

I showed up at the prescribed time at his front door, but I knew there was no way he was going up the mountain from the moment he opened the door. He looked like death warmed over. At some point in the past twenty-four hours, he had come down with some sort of flu. I offered to wait for him to get better even though I was dying to go up there. He knows me well enough to understand how much things like this mean to me, so he was gracious enough to tell me to go on ahead without him.

After getting instructions on how to get to where I need to go, I load up in my truck and take off towards my destination. I have to turn around and backtrack a few times, but it isn't too long before I find this new trail that my friend has scouted out. Granted, "trail" might be a bit of an exaggeration here. Really it is more of a shallow groove up the side of a mountain. To me, though, it looks like my next adventure. I roll my bike down out of the bed of the truck and grab my helmet off the passenger seat.

I start up the trail at a fairly safe pace at first since I'm not familiar with the area. Before long, the groove opens up a little bit, and

I am able to push my speed higher, and I get that familiar sensation of freedom that I love so much. Before long, I come up to a curve in the trail when I think I spot something through the trees.

I pull my bike over to the side of the trail and get off. I squint, trying to figure out what I'm seeing, but I just can't tell from this distance. It is about 100 yards down the side of the hill, so it takes me a bit to get down, but I realize what it is before I get to it. It is an abandoned vehicle. It looks like it has been here a while from the rust. All of the windows are broken, so the seats have started to rot away. I don't know how it was possible for this car to even get up here. I didn't see any road that it could take up here, and this was far from a four-wheel-drive vehicle.

I'm looking through one of the windows when I think I hear a voice off to my left. "Hello..."

I jerk up quickly and nearly knock myself silly from hitting my head on the car. It sounded like a little girl talking. I look around for the source of the voice, but I don't see anyone around me.

I decide to call out to whoever was out here with me. "Hello? Who's there?"

I don't get any response. I try again, but once again, the area remains quiet. All that I hear now is the sound of the leaves rustling in the wind. Between the trees and the sun beginning to set, it is starting to get dark out, and I'm starting to get more than a little freaked out. I decide it is time for me to leave.

As I turn, another voice calls out to me; this time, it sounds like a boy. "Please, don't leave us here."

I start spinning in slow circles, looking for anybody at this point. "Okay, this isn't funny. If someone is there, come out right now!"

Once again, though, my words don't bring anything but the sound of leaves in the wind. I've had enough of this place, and I start up the hill. I'm not going to stay another minute in this creepy place. Three minutes later, I'm on my bike and riding down the path towards my truck. It takes me about thirty minutes, but I've got my bike loaded up and am headed back towards my house. Even though I've got my music up loud, the sounds of the two voices seem to replay in my head. I just can't figure out what had happened up there.

Things were pretty normal that night and the next day. Nothing strange or unexplainable happened. Then it was like someone flipped a switch and things started happening that made me think I was going crazy. Doors would open and close on their own, chairs would rock with nobody sitting in them, even my fireplace tools would rattle around in their holder. That is just the start of it. I also am hearing knocking noises around the house, footsteps running about, and giggling.

This wasn't going on before I had been up on the hill. Somehow, I think that I have brought back home with me the two spirits that had spoken to me by the car. Even though I had no intention or desire for this to happen, I don't think I had a choice in the matter. So far, I don't think they mean me any harm, but I don't get the feeling they have any intention of leaving. I've thought about moving, but I'm sure they would just follow me to the next place too. I've tried to tell them to leave me alone, but it only seems to increase the activity like I've upset them somehow.

I guess there are only two choices, live with them or try and rid them somehow. It just is harder to push them away, seeing as I believe they are just kids. At some point, though, I think I'll have to get them to move on. Until then, though, I think I'm stuck with them.

10 UNKNOWN ENTITY

I'm haunted by a ghost. Yes, you heard me right, I am haunted. No matter where I go, this spirit, if that is what it is, follows me. I've had a number of paranormal experiences and believe that there are spirits all around us; we just can't always tell that they're there. This, though, is not just a fleeting vision of a shadow figure or an apparition that I've seen once or twice. I don't always sense its presence, but it's there, always. It has been with me since I was young, and as an adult, this entity has had a profound impact on my life.

It is impossible for me to fully describe what it is like to have something like this following you around for literally years. When it first started, it felt like I was going crazy. Things would go missing only to show up in strange places, my name being whispered into my ear when I'm the only one in the room, even strange bruises appearing all over my body like something has grabbed hold of me. How do you come to terms with something that you know exists but can't see or prove that it does? When you think you're the only sane person around you, does that really make it so?

I've been in three serious relationships in my life. I'm not saying that this being has been the only reason why they ended, but it definitely played a major role.

Whatever it is that is following me seems to be possessive of me for some reason. During the time I was dating or engaged to these men when we would share a bed together, there would be times where they would wake up to the feeling that they were being choked to death. As the occurrences of this piled up, I realized that this happened every time that we had some sort of argument in which I was extremely emotional. The problem was when they were attacked, it would cause another fight starting the cycle all over again.

At first, I tried to convince them and subsequently myself that they were suffering from sleep paralysis. This condition is caused by a chemical that is produced in the brain that is supposed to keep you from moving while you are dreaming. Some people can experience the effects of this chemical after they are awake, keeping them from moving and also give the sensation of being choked. It made sense, but to have all three of them suffer from the same condition. This didn't seem likely. Also, none of them had experienced this before dating me, and the two relationships that ended stopped suffering the symptoms after we split. I didn't blame them though, how can you be with someone when you are convinced your life may be in danger? This just seemed too coincidental for it to not mean something. In the end, I always knew what was causing it on some level, even from the beginning, but the desire to be happy was greater than my logic.

My current relationship, which I've been in for six years, is falling apart around me because of this. I've been honest about the entity that follows me with this man, and he knows I'm telling him the truth but even knowing the truth doesn't mean he accepts it or that he is willing to deal with it. In the end, I fear that I may be better off alone. At least it would be safer for everyone if I don't get involved with someone.

I wish I could say that I'm the only one that notices things going on, but that isn't the case. I know that I've gone to bed with all of the lights off in the house only to wake up around 2:00 am and have every single one of them on. I've found my front door wide open and unlocked when I check every door right before going to sleep. There are times when you walk into the room that the energy in the room will literally feel different, almost like it is thicker in one place than the rest of the house. All of these things others have seen firsthand. Nobody except my boyfriend is willing to spend the night at my house any longer. My mother is too scared to even set foot in my place. She's never said anything, and she never would, but she blames me for us not being close anymore.

I have gone to extraordinary lengths to rid myself of this thing. I've used salt, crystals, smudging, I've even had people from many different religions come out and bless my house and me, but nothing has worked. Whatever this thing is, it seems to be immune to the normal tactics of ridding an unwanted attachment. I even had to get rid of both of my pets because they would be freaking out constantly, either barking or hissing at empty corners or doorways. I knew they saw it, and I could not subject them to that kind of stress. It felt like I was torturing them.

Really, I just want it to go away. I want to be a normal

woman with a normal life rather than some sort of weird paranormal package deal. I want to be able to express what I'm feeling without fear that it might attack who I'm with. I don't think that is too much to ask. I will continue to do my research on ways to separate myself from this being who seems unwilling to move on. It's either that or just accept it as part of life, which I'm unwilling to do.

11 LOVE BEYOND LIFE

In my lifetime, I can honestly say that I had one true love. A person that made me feel more whole than I ever could on my own. It was so amazing the time we spent together; I guess that's what you get when the love of your life is also your best friend. Not everyone gets to experience that type of thing, but I wish they could. To find someone that will love you with all of their heart no matter what, that was something special. Sure, it took us a while to be able to realize what probably should have been obvious to us right away, but once our eyes were opened, there was no denying what was there.

I cherish the time my wife and I spent together; the memories I will have of our life together strengthens me even as I now lay alone in a bed far too big for just one person. After she passed away, it was like a light went out in my world. My family and my friends have encouraged me to find someone to share my remaining years with, but I'm not interested. I know she would want me to be happy, but when you've already found your soulmate, why would you settle for anything but that?

After being with someone for so long and then they're gone, you really start to take notice of the things that they did both alone, and you did as a couple. It isn't the grand events of our life that I tend to get choked up over but rather the simple things she did every day. I remember just enjoying the sight of her getting ready in the morning. She followed the same routine for the thirty-six years we spent together. She would sit in front of the mirror in our bedroom and brush her hair, then sprayed two pumps of perfume onto herself. That is where this ghost story begins, with a scent that I had almost forgotten.

I was getting ready to go over to the senior center to play a little bit of chess with one of the guys that I had met there recently. We both had lost our wives and enjoyed a game or two while enjoying each other's company. We never talked much about the women we had loved and lost. We didn't need to, but to have that kindred spirit who knew and had felt the profound emptiness was a source of strength we both needed. I was sitting on my bed trying to tie my shoes, cursing the pain and lack of flexibility that even such a remedial task caused me at my advanced age when out of nowhere, I smelled perfume. Without a doubt, I knew it was my wife's favorite. There was no doubt I had bought it for her for years, and I would know it anywhere.

Without even thinking about it, I looked over to the table where she kept her makeups and whatnot for years, expecting to see her sitting there gazing back at me out of the corner of her eye in the mirror. Though, all I see is the few odds and ends that I have placed on its surface. I had almost immediately gotten rid of her everyday items since they only served as a constant reminder of my loss. My heart sank with the reminder that she was gone, and I finished tying my shoes and left for the day.

Upon returning home, as soon as I walked into the bedroom, I knew something was different. The room felt fuller, more whole than it had since my wife had died. I only assumed that it was caused by the time I had spent with my friend for the last few hours. Was this what it felt like to "move on" like so many people had urged me to do? As nice as it felt to have a huge weight lifted ever so slightly, that was a constant reminder of my loneliness; it was what tied me to her.

I sat down on my bed and began the task of taking off my shoes. I was tired and wanted to take a bit of an afternoon nap, a regular occurrence these days. Kicking off my shoes, I laid down on what still was my side of the bed, which was closest to the door. I'd tried to move more to the center or even to her side as a way to ease the emptiness that I had felt early on but found I was unable to sleep anywhere but the place I had occupied for so long. I lay my head down against the pillow, and without warning, the smell of my wife's perfume fills my nose.

Tears burn my eyes and threaten to overflow from the familiar smell, but she is gone, and now my mind, in a moment of weakness, seems to be conjuring up the smell on its own as if it is trying to torment me. I rolled over to look to the side of the bed where she used to sleep, to the pillow she would lay her head on, and I have to blink with disbelief. The pillow appears to have been used like someone has laid down and put their head on it. I try to remember if I had maybe put my arm up and that had been the cause of the depression. I didn't think I had, and I didn't remember it being that way when I walked in, but I'm not sure I would have noticed anyway.

Somehow the perfume smell seems to be coming from the pillow. I picked it up and held it to my face, ready to inhale, knowing there is no way that it could be possible. But as soon as the air filled my lungs, there was no doubt that where the impression had been, the smell of perfume was evident. If I didn't know better, it was as if my wife had laid down right next to me. I knew it was impossible, but I was going to enjoy this delusion as long as I could. I held the pillow close to me and closed my eyes, and went to sleep. For the first time in over a year, I didn't wake up during the night to an empty bed having to remind myself she was gone.

Waking up in the morning, I put the pillow to my nose, trying to find some lingering scent from the night before, but all I smell is laundry detergent. Obviously, my waking memory is over, but I'm thankful for the pleasant reminder of the woman I love, even though she isn't here with me.

I walk into the bathroom and look at myself in the mirror. I need a shave, but it isn't like I'm trying to impress anyone, so I climb into the shower with the hopes of the warm water loosening my old joints. I've never taken long showers, so it isn't more than ten minutes, and I'm standing on the rug outside the tub drying myself off. I look down on the counter where the sink is to grab my hairbrush and see that my razor is sitting on the counter. I hadn't taken it out of the drawer since I had decided to skip scraping my face off for another day. After the night before, I couldn't help but remember my wife used to put it on the counter for me when she noticed my beard was getting long. She was a woman that always told me she liked how I looked cleanly shaven. It was a little nudge reminder that she would always give me. Somehow, I must have just grabbed it out of habit, and since it was on my mind because of last night, I shaved anyway.

After the last twelve hours, I was starting to get a little concerned with the things I was experiencing. At my age, anything could be a sign of an oncoming medical issue, and when you are delusional and forgetting things, the first thought that popped into my head was Alzheimer's. The thing that scared me the most was leaving the home that my wife and I had built together. I needed to schedule an appointment with my doctor, so I could get checked out. I just hoped nothing serious would happen until I could go in and see her.

Nearly a week had gone by with no strange happenings. The doctor had given me a clean bill of health, although I did receive a strange look or two when I told her about what had happened.

"You're just getting old, is all. Other than that, you're fine." Why is it that when the elderly start telling you weird things, the only reasoning behind it seems to be age makes you slow and crazy?

This is about the time when I started having dreams about her. Don't misunderstand that from time to time, I would see her while I slept, reliving some of our fondest moments together, but this was different. In my dreams, we would talk to one another about things that she hadn't been alive for or have any way of knowing about. She told me that she was with me in the home, that the perfume had been her, that she had laid next to me in the bed. They were so vivid, so real that I could hardly tell they were dreams other than when I would awaken the next morning.

Even my family made comments about how my mood was improving. The dreams brought me a closeness to her that I hadn't felt since the time she went into the hospital for the final time, never to come home again. It was like we were together again. I started looking for signs that the dreams were more than just that, visions of an unconscious mind. Everything seemed to be touched by her presence, I know that she didn't appear, but the house just seemed like home again. Love filled the inside, or maybe it was just me.

All question of whether it was my wife's spirit making itself known to me fell away when one day I found an object that I had put away soon after she died turned up on the table next to her side of the bed. It was her wedding ring, something that I had put away in a lockbox for safekeeping. Somehow it had been removed and placed in the exact spot where she had always put it before bed every night. My heart was filled with joy in this evidence that she is with me.

I haven't told my family what I'm seeing since I'm sure they would just tell me that I'm losing it and I am grieving in an unhealthy way. I know what the truth is; my wife and I's love is stronger than anything I thought possible. They say love conquers all; now I know it can at least conquer death.

For over a year, all I could think about was counting the days, hours, minutes, and seconds until we would finally see each other again. Maybe that is why the events of the past couple of weeks have been occurring. There are too many coincidences to ignore the possibility that the veil of death may not confine our love. Is it possible that our two souls are destined to be intertwined forever? It is a comforting thought to think that we share a love that will bridge lifetimes. I love her more than anything; no amount of time will ever be enough to be by her side, so I figured I'd start with forever.

12 BATH TIME

Recently I have moved back into the home where I grew up as a child. My father recently remarried, and they decided to move into her home in Washington state. Not wanting the place where I had so many good memories to go to a stranger, I convinced my wife that we should buy the place from him. We had been kicking around the idea of getting a bigger place, and this gave us the opportunity to do so without breaking the bank.

When I was growing up, I had always had "feelings" that I wasn't alone there. It always felt like someone was watching you no matter where you went, but it seemed to be the worst in the bathroom. I never saw anything there, so I just assumed it was an overactive imagination as I got older. I certainly wish that is what it really was, but after a few months of living in the house, we started experiencing things that made me regret the decision to return to my childhood home.

It really started one night when our son walked into our bedroom around 10:00 pm. I had been checking the scores for the day while my wife was reading a book. From the minute he walked into the room, I knew that something was wrong. His eyes were puffy, and you could still see the streaks the tears had left on his cheeks. He told us that he had heard splashing in the bathroom and strange voices. Neither one of us really thought much of this claim since he was predisposed to having nightmares, so it made sense that this was simply that.

I took his hand and walked him into the bathroom to show him that nothing was in there. He walked around the small room, exploring every possible place that someone could be hiding, which wasn't very many places before he seemed satisfied that there wasn't anyone there. I then took him back to his room and tucked him into bed.

A few nights later, I heard splashing noises coming from the bathroom. I assumed my wife was giving our son a bath, and he was just playing around. When I saw her sitting in the living room watching television, I was surprised. Our son was only five years old, and it didn't seem safe to leave him in the bath by himself, so I asked her why she had done so. She looked at me funny and said that he wasn't in the bath but playing in his room. I walked down the hall, and sure enough, he was there on the floor playing with his action figures.

Now I didn't know what to think. I know I had heard splashing coming from the bathroom. I didn't believe that I could have been mistaken. The sound was distinct. There didn't seem like anything else to do but go look. As soon as I opened the door, I stopped dead in my tracks. There was water everywhere; it looked like someone had been flailing around in a tub that was full of water. I just knew our son had done it while playing. I didn't like having these types of conversations, but I needed to tell him that this type of behavior was not acceptable.

I sat him down and tried to get him to admit to playing in the bathroom, but he just wouldn't tell me the truth. He kept saying it was "The Lady" that did it. He wasn't a child that had imaginary friends before, but a fake friend wasn't going to make a mess in the bathroom. I told him that he was going to help me clean up the water that he had gotten all over the floor. He threw a fit when I told him this telling me it wasn't fair to make him do it since he hadn't done anything wrong. This only frustrated me further because he just kept on lying.

The next day the three of us decided we were going to go to a movie together. It had been a little while since we had done this, and we all needed a little time out of the house. When we got back, I noticed footprints leading from the front of the house all the way down the driveway.

I told my wife and son to stay in the car while I cleared the house. I walked to the front door and checked the knob. It was still locked, which was strange. I mean, why would an intruder relock the door? Once the door was open, I investigated the family room. The footprints continued inside on the hardwood floor. My eyes fell upon the watery droplets trailing down the hallway.

I crept down the hall, every creak of the floorboards a groaning shriek in my ears. The path may lead away from here, but I'm not sure what could be waiting for me on the other side of the bathroom threshold. My hand shook as it neared the handle of the closed room. With my eyes squinted shut, I begged my inner self for the courage, my gut all-the-while telling me to turn back. However, this is my home, and I'll be damned if I'm going to be driven out of it.

After drawing in a deep, shivery breath, I flung the door open before I could change my mind. My eyes widened in horror at the scene in front of me. Every inch of the walls was covered in wet black handprints. My eyes darted around the room to the ceiling, where more prints were perched. I began to count the numerous prints for a moment, but honestly, there were just too many; it seemed like hundreds. Up until this point, the water on the ground had looked clear and clean, but this water was anything but. I backed out of the room using the doorframe for support, unable to take my eyes off the walls. My entire body was crawling with shudders. Only one thought remained in my head. I *have to get out of here.*

Memories of my youth flash back to my mind, where I felt eyes upon me every time I entered the room. Could it be possible that it wasn't my imagination? I run out of the house and slam the door behind me. I don't bother locking it; I just want to get the hell away from whatever was in that house. I leap into the driver's seat and slam the car into reverse. My wife starts asking me questions about what was going on, but I ignore her. There will be time to answer questions when we are safe.

We never went back to the house. I hired a cleaning crew to go in and make the house presentable for sale. We stayed in a hotel for a few weeks while we found a new place to live. Childhood memories be damned; someone else can have the house.

13 BICYCLE SIGHTING

Although personally, I have never had any experiences with ghosts or any other paranormal entity in my life, I wanted to share a story that happened to my brother while he was living in Ohio during the mid-2000s. This experience landed him in the hospital with a strange illness for over a week. The doctors couldn't really tell us what was wrong with him, only that it seemed as if his organs were shutting down for some reason. Fortunately, the disease, if that is what it really was, seemed to vanish as quickly as it came. To this day, he believes the events of a single night are what caused him to get sick. This is his story.

During the warmer months of the year, my brother liked to ride his bike to and from work every day. He owned a car, but with his busy schedule, this was really the only time he had to be physically active on a daily basis. It was his "workout" as he called it. Most nights, he would be getting home around 10:00 at night, so the return trip home was done in the dark. Really there isn't a lot of traffic on the road, so the only real obstacle that he has to look out for is the train tracks. If you don't pay attention, it is easy to lose control and crash. I know this from personal experience.

It was September 2006, and as he tells it, there wasn't anything unusual about the ride. He was just about to make it to the tracks when he noticed a person with their back to him standing in the middle of the road holding a bicycle of their own. Although he could have just avoided them by going around in either direction, he decided that he would stop and make sure they were okay.

Obviously, it isn't normal for a person to be blocking the road like this in the middle of the night, so he decided to call out to them instead of walking right up and possibly getting into a situation that could be dangerous. From what he could tell, it was a guy that was standing there. You have to understand that my brother is a pretty big guy and the person that he described in the road was small of stature, but you never can be too careful sometimes.

"Hey, are you alright? Do you need any help?"

The person didn't even move; it was like they hadn't heard him yell to them. He tried again, louder this time, but once again, there wasn't any sign that they had even registered there was another person around. There always was a train that came by at night, so he wanted to make sure the person was going to be okay to leave alone, so he figured he didn't have a choice but to approach them.

As he walked towards them, he kept calling out to no avail. The guy just stood there, motionless. As he got closer, he described feeling a nervous energy going through him and goosebumps prickled his arms. The feeling only got stronger, the closer he got. He considered just jumping back on his bike and riding by, but he couldn't in good conscience just leave the guy here all alone.

Finally, he managed to reach where the guy was standing

and decided to try tapping him on the shoulder to get his attention. As soon as his finger made contact, the "person" snapped around inhumanly fast. My brother was horrified by what he saw. The skin on the face was a bloodless white that didn't completely cover the things skull beneath. It was obvious to him from the moment he saw it that this thing wasn't alive.

My brother tried to take a couple of steps back, but in fear, his feet jumbled together, and he fell to the ground. The creature advanced on him quickly. Lying on his back on the hard pavement, he stared into the milky vacant eyes, sure that he was taking his last breaths. He squeezed his eyes shut, unwilling to look at the nightmare mere feet in front of him. He describes a cold, clammy hand running down his face and chest. Where it touched, a burning cold feeling is felt then the fingers feel like they are drawn away.

Eyes still closed; he waits for what happens next. He described to me a bright light shining through his eyelids. He hears a door slam shut behind him and risks opening his eyes. The specter is no longer there. He hears someone running up to him and flinches when they come into view.

They think he has crashed his bike and were stopping to make sure he didn't need any help. He didn't want to sound crazy, so he just went with the story that he had not been paying attention and had lost control when going over the tracks, but he was okay to ride the rest of the way home. He thanked them, and they drove off, leaving my brother alone.

He rode the rest of the way home, but he had already begun to feel ill. When he walked in the door, and we laid eyes on him, he looked really bad. He looked pasty and was sweating profusely. He was unsteady on his legs and collapsed onto the couch when he got near it. After he wouldn't respond to his name other than moaning, we decided he needed to go to the hospital.

As I said before, it was over a week before he was released. During his stay, he relayed to the family about his encounter with the ghoul on the road. All of us believe when that thing touched him, it was trying to kill him. None of us doubted his story, he wasn't the type to make up something like this, and the speed in which he got sick further convinced us that this wasn't a normal illness.

After he was released from the hospital, my brother never rode his bike anywhere near the tracks again. He would go out of his way in order to avoid crossing them at that point. I can't say that I blame him; next time, he may not be so lucky.

14 THE TALL ONE

To start with, it is important that you know that I consider myself a psychic medium. From the time I was about eight, I started to see and hear things that no one, especially someone my age, should. By this, I mean I could see and communicate with people that had crossed over. The first time it happened, I was terrified, but as I got older, it somehow managed to become almost normal. Sometimes they don't even know I'm there, but most just want to talk, to relay messages to loved ones. As odd as it sounds, they're just like, well, people, just dead.

When I was going to college, I met my best friend. We were immediately drawn to each other because she was a psychic. When we were together, it just seemed like our abilities were taken to another level entirely. We could communicate and talk and pick up on things so much more clearly than we could ever do so alone. When we both graduated, after much debate, we decided that we wanted to live together. It wasn't that we thought we would be bad roommates, but we both had to decide if we wanted to be close all the time, given what it could mean with our abilities.

I had always just relied on my natural abilities to communicate with those who had passed before. One night my friend suggested that we try something different. I had always been wearying of Ouija boards because if you weren't careful, there was no telling what or who you would be inviting to communicate with you. Really, I wasn't interested in doing this because I just saw it as a lesser version of what I could already do. On the other hand, auto writing gave the spirit a chance to use your hand to communicate a message directly. Although some consider this a more dangerous thing to do because you are allowing something into yourself, it is also a more personal connection with the spirit you are channeling. I had always wanted to try it, and with my friend's help, I was confident that we would get something to come through.

We decided that it would be best if I did the writing since I was more used to communicating with spirits. After opening myself up to them, I got a strong feeling that someone was eager to speak to us. The image in my head was of a man, he was tall, probably over six feet, and he was dressed like someone out of the 1800s. During the session, he was very kind and openly answered all of our questions that we had. He didn't remember how he had died or what age he was, but from the picture in my head, I would say mid-forties is likely.

After dismissing him, I got the distinct impression that although he was no longer able to use my body to communicate with us, he was reluctant to leave. I felt that he had been alone for so long that he was desperate to hold on. It was so sad that I started to cry. I don't know if they were my tears or if I was feeling his emotions through me. I'm guessing a little bit of both.

Over the next few weeks, I would see him everywhere I went. My roommate and I even did another auto writing session with him. This time he used her to write. At some point, he reached out with her hand and touched mine. It was an oddly intimate gesture from the spirit. I'd never felt such powerful emotion before. To best describe it, I would say it was love, but that of a close friend.

Not everything he did, though, was welcome. When I was at work, and I didn't recognize his presence, he would move things around on my desk. I had to tell him to stop doing that. He seemed to get the point and cut this out. Me, I was used to this type of thing, but if someone else had seen it, there was a chance that they would have been pretty scared.

One of the best times we had together though is when I

would be listening to music. It didn't matter if it was at home or driving in the car; the guy loved music. Joy would literally radiate off of him when it was playing. I couldn't help but be in a good mood when this was going on.

Up until this point, I have never come into contact with a spirit that is so connected to me on such a personal level. He has become a friend to me, a constant companion. When you allow a spirit into yourself, neither one of you has secrets from the other. You are connected in a way that not many people can understand or ever really experience. I know I have heard of people having spirits both good and bad attach themselves to them. I think that is what has happened here. But I have to admit too that I am also attached to him. If he were to leave, it would be no different than losing a close friend.

Haunted Objects:

**Real Creepy Stories of
Paranormal Items**

MERGING TRAFFIC

People like to collect all kinds of things, dolls, stamps, even cars. Me, I collected street signs. I didn't have two that were alike and was always looking to add something new to my collection. Some of them were pretty old and hard to come by. The ones that seemed to be the most sought after were ones that had been involved in some kind of traffic accident. The worse the accident, the more the sign was sought after and thus was worth it. A lot of times, you have to be really lucky to find them on the side of the road or be in the right place at the right time when the pole a sign is on gets taken out by a car.

One of the more modern signs I didn't have was one that had a merging traffic symbol on it. For some reason, this simple sign would illude me time and time again. I started to think that I may never get one, then tragedy struck one day when I was getting on the freeway. A car crossed in front of a semi, and with the difference in weight, there was only going to be one outcome. The compact car bounced off the front bumper and flipped six or seven times before coming to rest in the ditch. Parts of the car were strewn all over the road from the deadly rollover.

I knew I was going to be late getting to work since I was now stuck where I was at. Traffic had come to a standstill, and we weren't going anywhere anytime soon. A glint of yellow caught my eye in the weeds on the side of the road. I just figured it was a standard speed limit sign or interstate label, but I figured what the heck, I'm stuck anyways.

I was peppered by insults from people upset that I was getting out of my car on the freeway, but when you have a chance to get a sign, you make your move. As I got closer, I realized it wasn't what I had originally thought it was. I looked down, and I had to blink a couple of times to make sure I was seeing things correctly. Here it was, the sign I had been searching for, the *Merging Traffic* sign.

I picked it up, looking carefully at it. Even though the post had been bent in all different directions, the sign was intact. It was a stroke of good luck. I took my wrench out of my back pocket and unscrewed the sign from the bent pole, and hefted it back to my car.

I sat there for more than an hour before the traffic started to move again, but even that couldn't dampen my good mood.

I spent all day thinking of where the perfect place would be to put the new addition to my collection. When my workday was finally over, and I pulled into my garage, I left the sign in the back seat until I was ready to wash and mount it. I went to my bedroom to change when I heard my car alarm going off. It took me by surprise since I hadn't locked the doors, so the alarm shouldn't have even been activated. My car was pretty new, so I didn't think that it could have a short in the system yet, so I figured I better go take a look.

I went to the door to the garage, and as soon as I twisted the handle, the alarm went silent. I walked out into the garage with my key fob and locked and unlocked the car so the alarm would for sure be off. Since I was out there, I grabbed the new sign out of the back seat and carried it into my bedroom. I have the walls adorned with a number of road signs, and I figured that since I had sought out this one for so long that it would be nice to be able to look at it. The signs require special mountings that I would have to go to the hardware store the next day for before I could do anything with it so it would stay on the floor for the night.

After a quick dinner and a few hours of television, I was ready to go to sleep. I usually get to sleep early, but I couldn't seem to get comfortable. My entire left side of my body ached. Finally, after an hour of tossing and turning, I got up to take a couple of aspirin for the pain. Whether it was from the pills or exhaustion, I finally drifted off about an hour later.

I found myself behind the wheel. I had this overwhelming sense that I had to get to where I was going quickly or something bad would happen. I would need to push it. I sped down the on-ramp, not even bothering to check for oncoming traffic. I only cared about what was in front of me; the people behind wouldn't catch me.

The car quickly gains speed as I near the merge area, and it looks like I have managed to find an empty spot to turn into. I press the gas to get to freeway speed and turn the wheel. Unfortunately, I don't see the shadow blocking the sun until it is too late. The front of my car is clipped by the front of the massive truck, and I lose all control. I see sky then pavement over and over again as the car flips time and time again. I feel a terrible pain on my left side but am too disorientated to know why. I hear a crash and crunching noise above me; then, everything goes black.

I shot up in bed and winced. The pain on my left side from earlier was far worse than it had been, and my head was killing me. The dream had seemed so vivid and real. The terror I felt when the crash was going on was still with me. I hear footsteps next to the bed, but there is no one there. The sign falls over with a loud metallic crash, and the footsteps walk out the door and down the hall.

I sat there, not sure what had just happened. I believed ghosts could exist, especially when people died under tragic circumstances. First, there had been the alarm, then the pain, the car wreck dream, and then the sign falling over after hearing footsteps walk over to it from the bed. I looked over at the back of the sign that now lay flat on my bedroom floor. The only thing that made sense was that the man had died in the car crash I had seen earlier. Had he been drawn to the sign I had brought home?

I now believe that this was the case. I think he was telling me that my precious sign came at a price, and even though I didn't have any part in it, I profited from his death. I thought about getting rid of it, but I just couldn't do it. I like to think of it as a memorial to him. I just hope the man has found peace.

CRIB OF SORROW

I have a sister that lost her 5-month-old son to SIDS (*Sudden Infant Death Syndrome*). Unfortunately, not a lot is known about the causes of SIDS; for certain, there have been many theories. Our entire family was devastated by Caleb's passing, and I believe that negative energy is what drew a negative spirit to us and nearly caused the death of my sister's then infant daughter.

Kennedy was a beautiful baby. She relit the hope and love that my sister lost when Caleb was taken at far too early of an age. There was a time when I doubted that I would ever see the woman that my sister used to be again. There was nothing that could have been done to prevent what had happened, but she blamed herself for the death. All that changed when she found out that she was pregnant. It was like the purpose of caring for her unborn child gave her direction and hope that hadn't been there before.

Her thinking was that having the same crib that Caleb did would give Kennedy a connection to her brother. The bed was repainted with a pink color instead of the dark blue that it had been before to go with the remodeled nursery. One week after she was born, Kennedy came home, and after a quiet month, something went horribly wrong.

A normally quiet and happy baby, Kennedy would sleep most of the night without much fussing. She was a baby most parents would dream of. One night though, when my sister put her in her crib, she began shrieking at the top of her lungs. She would shake and turn blue like she couldn't breathe, but as soon as she took her into any other room in the house, she would calm almost immediately and regain her normal coloring.

My sister suspected that something was wrong with the crib. She even spent a night sleeping in it, trying to see if whatever was wrong with it would happen to her but with no success. Despite nothing happening, she became more and more convinced something was wrong with the crib. She was terrified that if she kept it that she would lose Kennedy as she did Caleb.

My sister is a very religious woman, and when she turned to her church for help, she was afraid that it wouldn't stop if she just got rid of the crib, so she wanted to make sure the house was safe for her daughter. Some of the church elders came the next day to see what was happening and if they could help. They tried to get Kennedy to go into the crib peacefully, but even when they placed her inside, she began to shriek and turn the same blue color as always. They prayed around the crib, but her cries seemed to intensify, and she seemed to be going from blue to purple.

The elders had seen enough to believe some sort of evil entity had attached itself to the bed, and in order to purify it, they had to burn it completely. Even though it was early afternoon and a bright sunny day, I don't ever remember being more scared than I was at that time. They brought the crib outside and sprinkled it with oil to bless it, then doused it in another type of oil used to light furnaces. What came next is something that I couldn't have imagined. The crib wouldn't burn; it was on fire, I could see the red and orange flames licking its surface and the intense heat coming off of it, but it refused to be turned to ash.

It took the elders multiple gallons of oil and several hours to completely consume the crib. The priest believed that a demon or evil spirit had attached itself to the item and wanted to torture Kennedy. He believed it was attracted to the terrible events surrounding Caleb's death. It saw the happiness my sister had rediscovered in her daughter and wanted to use that love to inflict pain.

I believed what the elders thought had happened. I had heard stories of spirits coming into people's homes when they bought them at garage sales or secondhand stores, but I didn't know that it could happen to something that was associated with tragedy. It makes me question what is safe to keep and what I should throw away because I don't know what or who I might be inviting in.

ONE HECK OF
A RIDE

If someone had asked me before my experience if I believed in ghosts or spirits of some kind, I probably would have told them, "Yeah, I guess," or "Maybe...". I wasn't a skeptic but never having come into contact with anything of the sort forced it into the realm of the hypothetical. But sometimes, hypothetical can come up and smack you right upside the head when you least expect it. That is what happened to me on three successive nights riding home on a bike I just purchased from a secondhand store.

I was coming home late from work one evening. I was a person who liked to get his exercise any way that I could, so given that it wasn't very far, I rode my bike to and from work each day. That night it seemed particularly dark out, so much so that I was having trouble seeing the road even with the assistance of the light strapped to the handlebars. A new moon did nothing to help the situation, leaving me with only a small glow on the road ahead.

I tend to ride pretty quickly, pushing myself to reach fairly high speeds on my bike, so I was a little surprised when I felt a tug on the back of my shirt. I looked over my shoulder and didn't see anyone there. Not only that, but there also wasn't a light or anything to indicate that another rider was near me. At the speed I was going, it was also unlikely that someone would be able to grab me either, and most concerning was that if I couldn't see anyone, how could they see me?

The start gave me the motivation to push a little harder to get home as quickly as I could. I pushed hard down on the pedals to accelerate when the front wheel on my bike suddenly stopped, not like breaking stopped, but no motion at all. I felt myself pitch forward and a sudden feeling of weightlessness then over the handlebars I went, followed by a brief slide across the ground. I looked up, and I saw a car coming in my direction, and although close to me, I had time to move out of the way despite the aching cuts and bruises that I was sure was forming.

Leaning next to my bike, I looked it over, trying to figure out what had caused the wheel to suddenly stop. The bike still looked like it was okay. I seemed to take the worst of the impact, and other than a few scrapes, I felt fine. Grabbing hold of the wheel, I assumed that it would be stuck fast, but it spun freely as if nothing had happened just a minute before. I meticulously maintain my bike, seeing how it is my transportation to and from work. Even though I had just bought this bike used recently, I knew every moving part on it, so I wasn't sure what had happened. I gave everything a once over and decided nothing was out of place, so I rode the rest of the way home, although in a slight bit of discomfort.

The next day I felt the wreck more than I had when it had happened. My elbow was sore where I had hit it, and the scabs where the road had cut me pulled against the skin with every pedal. As was my usual routine, I was coming home late down the same road that I had taken my spill the night before. Thinking that if someone was messing with me the night before, they would do it again near the same place. Fortunately, nothing happened, and I breathed a sigh of relief when I turned onto the road leading to my house.

I thought that I was going to make it home without incident when the front tire on my bike halted again. I must have felt something going wrong, or it could have just been dumb luck because I didn't get flipped off my bike this time. I looked around the street trying to find my assailant, but the street was empty. I didn't even hear the sound of someone running away into the darkness.

I was angry at what were a number of options. First, if someone was doing this to me, I could have been seriously hurt twice now. Secondly, at myself, if I had missed something on the bike that was causing some sort of malfunction, then I was to blame. I committed myself to pouring over every inch of the bicycle when I got home. I remounted the bike and began peddling toward my house.

I pulled into my driveway and walked up to the keypad next to the garage door and punched in the combination to open the door. I pull my bike into the garage and put it up on the stand, where I do all of my maintenance and repairs. I spend the next three hours taking apart everything on the bike, applying grease and lubricant, and adjusting every cable and lever on it. Nothing stands out with the wheels or the gears that would cause the failure on the road. I hadn't seen anyone there, though, and I didn't find anything wrong with the bike, so I didn't understand what was going on. But a thought in the back of my mind was starting to take shape. Something that I didn't want to accept, let alone consider.

Riding home the next night, I am extra cautious. I don't ride nearly as fast, so I don't wreck no matter what happens. My head is on a swivel looking for anyone or anything in the road that would cause my wheel to stop. Things go pretty normally until I get about halfway home. I have to ride down a pretty steep hill and stand up on the pedals to give myself a little natural shock absorption. As soon as my weight was on it, the pedals gave out. My feet drop to the ground, and the bike is sent off-balance, flipping over a curb.

My chest impacts first, and it knocked the wind from my lungs. My head bounced off the ground, and the world went black. I come to pretty quickly, but I am in an immense amount of pain. I just sit there for probably 15 minutes, just trying to get the road to stop spinning. I knew I have a concussion and was hoping that the throbbing in my wrist was just a sprain and not a broken bone.

The pain is almost unbearable, just dragging myself and what remains of my bike to the side of the road. I am still trying to shake off my head impacting the pavement, as I try to assess what had just happened. The pedal arm had completely come off, and the sprocket had rotated opposite the normal direction it turned with the axle, which for those of you who don't know bikes, is almost impossible without a tool to do so. I grabbed hold of it and tried to rotate it back, but it wouldn't move. I looked down to where my pedals used to be, and it looked as if something had melted right through the arm.

I looked around, trying to find anything in the road that could have caused the wreck, but all I could find were tiny pieces of broken reflectors and the two pieces of what used to be the pedals. No one was around, no cars, no people. It just didn't seem possible. Three days in a row, all by myself with nothing mechanically wrong with the bike and all three days the bike malfunctions, and now here it sits with the sprocket rotated the wrong way and the pedals severed.

The thought that had started to take hold the night before came front and center in my mind. I had heard of entities attaching themselves to objects before. Was it possible that this was the cause of the problems that I was having? I didn't know for sure, and frankly, I wasn't willing to test the theory. I was done with this bike. Whether it was haunted or just some kind of jinx, I wouldn't ride it again.

To this day, I'm unsure of the cause of the three accidents on the route back home from my work. I threw the bike out, not really caring if it was a waste of money or not. Better out a few bucks than dead, I figured. I went out and bought my next bike new. I figured I would be safe; that way, if some sort of entity was attached to a used bike, this was the safest bet. So far, everything is going well. I hope it stays that way.

LIGHTS OUT

One of the worst parts of working in a hospital is when a person dies. Especially when it is one of the patients that you have gotten close to. This is especially the case for me, who works in the cancer wing. You see all kinds of people of all ages dealing with this horrible disease, and you spend months watching them go through the worst pain of their lives trying to fight back. Unfortunately, not all of them win. When this happens, one of the worst parts of my job is to take the person's body down to the morgue. After what happened to me one night, the lines I thought existed between the living and the dead changed forever.

I looked down at the face that just a few hours ago was contorted in such pain as her body shut down. I know she was scared to die, but she had accepted it and had a chance to say goodbye to the ones that were most important to her. It still is amazing to me how many people that are about to cross over are the ones who are comforting those that they will leave behind. But now her fight is done, and the pain she had experienced is in the past.

I lifted the white sheet over her and maneuvered around to the end of the gurney. As I pushed the cart down the hall, I see people looking at me out of the corner of their eyes. It isn't just the patients or their families but other staff too.

Susan had been here for three weeks as her body failed her. But she had been here multiple times, going through chemo and any other therapy in a desperate attempt to save her life. None had worked, though, and the people in the wing would miss her. She was one that people would say, "Susan is gonna beat this, look how hard she is fighting." But in the end, that wasn't the case.

I reached the elevator, and Tish, who was going down with me to the morgue, hit the button to call for the elevator. It took only a few seconds, and the chime announced the car's arrival. The doors opened, and I saw a few people filing out onto the floor. All of them gave the bed a wide berth as if the woman on the bed carried some sort of deadly virus. Hospitals are dedicated to treating the sick and wounded, and when that doesn't happen, the ones who have dedicated their lives to saving them take it the hardest. Some doctors don't even want to be around a dead person, thinking that somehow their streak of saving people will be jinxed. I pushed Susan into the elevator, and behind me, Tish hit the button for the basement.

The elevator jumped to life and began its descent into the bowels of the building. The bed rattled from the jostling of the sudden movement of the elevator, and I gripped the handles a little tighter to make sure it didn't roll around. I watched the numbers on the red LED panel reduce until the letter B was displayed. I heard the chime once again, and the doors slid open to a long white hallway.

Tish walked out first, so it would be easier for me to get the bed out of the elevator. She turned around to make sure I didn't need any help as I began to push.

Suddenly the lights in the elevator flickered slightly, and when I only had the bed halfway out, the door began to close. Unable to do anything about it, I just let go of the bed, and the doors hit both sides at the same time. Fortunately, the emergency lever popped the doors open again without damaging the elevator or the bed itself.
"That was weird," I told Tish.

"Yeah, this place down here gives me the creeps," she said back to me.

I grabbed back onto the handles and pushed the bed through the opening without any further problems. Our footsteps echoed down the empty hall as I continued with the grizzly journey. Tish reminded me that she had put the body into the morgue the last time, so it was my turn to do it.

"Great, I get to push the bed and put her away. It must be my lucky day," I replied with an obviously fake smile.

To get to the morgue, you have to push the body up a ramp before you get to the large swinging metal door. I lean into the bed and push a little harder to get up the incline. Tish and I set the brakes on the wheels, and I grab the handle and pull. The door makes a popping noise as the seal is broken into the room. The room itself is fairly small, and the first thing you notice is the smell. It is terrible, formaldehyde, and slow decay. It was a good thing I hadn't eaten anything recently because the stench was especially vile that day.

I pushed the bed in containing Susan's body all the way to the back of the freezer. A loud thunk announced that I had gotten it all the way in. The cold inside the room sent goosebumps up and down my arms as I turned around to leave, wanting to get out of there. As I went to leave, the door to the room swung shut, encasing me in the freezing cold.

"Tish! This isn't funny! Let me out!" I yelled through the door. The lights flickered, and then half of them went out. I reached over to flick the switch off and on, but the other half of the lights refused to come back on. I banged on the door with my fist, letting Tish know that I didn't think this was funny and to let me out. I heard a muffled noise on the other side of the door but couldn't make out what it was that she was saying. I heard a ticking noise coming from behind me. I looked up to the fan in the vent, thinking that it is the source of the noise, but the fan blade wasn't moving.

"Huh? That's weird..." I said to the empty room.

Suddenly it feels like the room drops at least 10 degrees. The tapping noise began to get louder and more insistent. I looked around, trying to find out where the noise was coming from. It sounded like something striking metal, but the only thing metal in the room was the drawers holding the bodies. The ticking noise starts again. It was coming from the drawers, but I didn't know how that could be. The only thing in there would have been another body.

I walked over to the drawer and put my ear right next to it, trying to see if, in fact, that was where it was coming from, but the noise refused to cooperate. I walked back to the door, ready to start my protests to Tish all over again. As soon as my open palm hit the door once, the entire room went black. Without light, you couldn't see six inches in front of your face, so I put my back to the door as that way, I at least knew where I was. I began slapping the door over and over again as the dark squeezed in around me.

"Help me, please help me," a female voice in front of me whispered.
"Tish! Tish, get me out of here!" I yelled. Tears of fear and panic stung my eyes and face as they trickled down my face in the cold. Someone or something was in there with me, and I was almost thankful I couldn't see what was speaking to me. I heard a dragging noise coming toward me on the floor, and I felt something touch my foot. I recoiled onto one leg, trying to get away from what was right beneath me.

"Tish! Please!" I sobbed. The unseen thing below me grabbed hold of my leg and felt like it was pulling itself up my body. I slapped my hand again and again on the door, trying to get her to open the door. Its hand was near my stomach, and I clenched my eyes tightly shut, hoping not to see the phantom. The next thing I know, I am falling backward, a brief moment of weightlessness, and then pain as my head hits the floor. At first, I think that whatever had been on me has pulled me to the ground, but I hear Tish's voice above me.

"Hey, are you okay? The door wouldn't open, it got stuck," she said.

I reached up to touch the back of my head, and I felt the beginnings of a nasty bump where my head had hit the ramp. My eyes dart to the freezer, looking for whatever had been in there, but the room was empty, and all the lights were on. There was no way I had hallucinated the entire thing, at least I didn't think so, but all that was in the room was the bed that I had just pushed in.

"I need to get out of here now," I told her.

"What are you talking about?" she looked at me.

"I need to get out of here right now," I said with a little more force.
She cocked an eyebrow up at me, then turned and shut the door. "You're acting weird," she said back, "Let me look at that bump on your head."

"I'm fine, let's just go, please," I shooed her off with a hand.

It took everything I had not to run straight to the elevator that night. But I can tell you the sense of relief I felt when I got back to our floor was like a huge weight had been lifted off my chest. I will not go down there alone to this day. I found out later that I'm not the only person who has had experiences down there, but until that night, I wouldn't have believed them if they had told me. I try to pass off the duty to take the bodies of our patients down there any time I can, but luckily for me, nothing has happened again. I just hope it stays that way.

FROM THE AUTHOR

At any early age I knew I noticed things that others did not. That I had a sensitivity about me that I could not quite explain.

I loved all horror movies, paranormal movies or shows and grew to love what some others just didn't care to understand.

Through the years I have come to realize that I am what they call "an empath". I feel things that others don't. It could be a place, a thing, a location, or someone talking to me and I just know more is going on then what they claim.

Honestly, I do not do much about this in my life. I've learned to deal with it, and not use it for anything other than knowledge.

I have lived in two haunted houses. This got me interested in the paranormal world and to seeking answers of all shapes and kinds.

I recently started a podcast and we discuss almost everything paranormal, mysterious or unknown. Feel free to take a listen and share your own ghost experiences with us as well!

Forever Haunted Podcast

The Ghosts That Haunt Me with Eve Evans Podcast

A Truly Haunted Podcast

Follow Eve S. Evans on instagram @eves.evansauthor

R. Harrell has always been fascinated by the paranormal. He enjoys the suspense of all things that go bump in the night.

Recently after beginning his writing career, he has noticed some odd unexplainable things start to happen. Mostly seeing figures out of the corner of his eye that disappear when he glances over or the feeling of being touched. On occasion a dream that has a sinister twist.

R. Harrell is co-writing numerous anthologies with Eve in the near future as he also plots a book of his own. A collection of terrifying horror stories with a planned release of 2020-early 2021.

R. Harrell and Eve met fifteen years ago and were instant best friends, inseparable mostly. After reading some of Eve's books he was intrigued and started writing some of his own stories. After that, the rest is pretty much history. They now enjoy co-writing ghostly anthologies based on true stories and don't plan on stopping anytime soon.

Printed in Dunstable, United Kingdom